Handlebars

Handlebars

Written by:
Steven Prouse

New Gondor Creations
West Columbia South Carolina

Dedicated to my boys.
We have within us all a hero and a villain.
The key to inner peace is to strive to be our hero selves.

Do your best to empathize with and uplift others
despite their differences, stand by the meek as they face
a hostile world, and strive to do no harm.

If you pursue these virtues, those who see only your vices
will ultimately be proven wrong.

My love and respect is forever yours.

Look at me, look at me
Hands in the air like it's good to be
Alive, and I'm a famous rapper
Even when the paths are all crookedy

-- The Flobots

<u>Chapter 1</u>

I stand in the large window looking out across the lawn, past the iron gates, and to the streets beyond. The men and women sitting behind me have been running me through various scenarios and contingencies crying apocalyptic, but all I can think of is that woman pushing the stroller down the sidewalk. I wonder if the baby in there is as ugly as she is. I wonder what sort of life it'll have growing up so ugly. Weak. Would it overcome? Would it grow into the strength that I have?

The wind blows the woman's hat. I enjoy watching her scramble while trying to hold the stroller still. The scene very nearly plays like a Three Stooges bit. A man grabs the hat before it flies into traffic. He hands it to her with a smile and moves on. She pops the hat back on her head, says something to the child in the stroller, and continues walking.

As my team awaits my response, my mind wanders to my own childhood. I was born to lower middle-class parents in a small southern town. To this day, I don't believe the town has a stop light.

I can't say that it was a good childhood. It was a childhood filled with strife. Weakness. Ignorance.

***

The blanket of ignorance and weakness came from a father who constantly needed to exert dominance over a child through violence and intimidation. Growing up as an only child in that home showed me how weakness manifests as stupid intimidation and violence. I didn't know it then, but the need to make myself small and inconspicuous, the need to be forgotten, taught me the true nature of power. I learned to control my environment. To control those around me. To manipulate my

surroundings through the superiority of intellectual might.

But not at eleven.

At eleven, I found excuses to stay at school because I was too terrified to go home.

It's easy to get perfect attendance awards when you'd rather be deathly ill in class than playing at home.

The tiny town in which I came of age only had two schools: elementary and high school. So, my sixth-grade year was my last year in elementary and, still feeling like a child, I would be thrown into high school life. I was on the edge of a precipice as this school year neared its end. For me, that precipice was on the edge of a dark, hopeless chasm where every milestone along a young man's path was damned to be dominated by a failed man who could only succeed through the destruction of others.

My father was a farmer. I mean, he worked at the convenience station down the street through the middle of the day when it was typically too hot to work outside. But most of his time through the mornings and evenings into late night were spent working around the house. My mom worked a standard day shift at a chicken hatchery.

That meant my every day through the summer was dominated by this man dangerously angry with his life. I hated the last day of school each year. I would turn twelve over that summer. Officially a pre-teen. I was leaving one school as the smallest kid in the oldest grade and entering a new school as the smallest kid in an ocean of adolescents. Between these two realities was the terror of a summer in the joy vacuum of my childhood home.

But there was something else that would shape that summer and save me from that hell.

Louis Bryant moved to town.

My hometown was a small one in central South Carolina. Town center was a grid of just a few roads lined with small, single-family homes, a town park, a volunteer fire station, two convenience stores, and the two schools. Apart from my family and one or two more on the other side of town, most of the town residents were older. Their kids had mostly moved away. Apart from Mrs. Shealy's home-based daycare, there weren't any younger kids in town. Most of my classmates lived in the overflow area from the larger city… the moneyed, lake side of town.

It was a good set up for the rich white kids. They didn't have to attend the larger, more urban schools. It practically functioned as a private school for the privileged who's primary inconvenience were the poor black and white kids with family ties to the surrounding farms. Mayberry before it found meth.

So, when I say Louis Bryant moved to town, it was a big deal.

His dad landed a foreman job at the hatchery. It was upward mobility for him, but it didn't pay enough for him to buy a house near the lake. Instead, he bought the Braxton's old house on the corner a few blocks down that had just come up for sale because the Braxtons moved across the country. Louis started sixth grade in my homeroom class at the beginning of the fourth quarter.

He was immediately the most popular kid in the class simply by virtue of being new. And attractive. The girls loved him. So, the guys loved him.

His house was across from the school. Since I walked home as slowly as I could, I often saw him walking home at the end of the day.

The last nine weeks of the school year passed without Louis and I exchanging a single word.

That summer began like any other. The day after school was out, I was expected to be up at dawn to help around the farm and to endure the resulting barrage of insults associated with how I couldn't do anything right. When the hell morning was done, my dad showered and ran off to work his day shift leaving me, at eleven, alone to fend for myself. The relief that came with his daily absence remains one on my fondest childhood memories. I knew the night would come and I'd be doing my best to avoid him and cling to my mother's side, but the day was mine.

Once I was alone, the house seemed more a prison than Fortress of Solitude. After retrieving a few dollars my mother had slipped me after chores, I hopped on my bike and hit the sidewalks. I headed to the small store where my father wasn't working. They had one of those spinning wire racks filled with comic books. I grabbed this month's Superman and a soda. Then I rode my bike to the town park behind the library.

The day was hot and the sun unforgiving, so I set up shop at one of the covered picnic tables and began to read. Apart from a car passing every now and then, the day was silent. I didn't know who the park was for since there really weren't any kids in town, but it felt like it was just for me.

The hot breeze blew. On a few occasions, it was timed perfectly to turn the pages for me. Most of the other times, I fought to keep the pages down as I journeyed with John Byrne and Superman on their Return to Krypton. Hawkman and Hawkwoman ship Supes back to Krypton where he hallucinates that his people didn't fail in saving themselves from a very real threat. It was totally ridiculous and fun. But wasn't that what Superman was?

"You're Quinn, right?"

His voice startled me.

I looked up and saw Louis astride his bike watching me read. He was maybe five feet from me. I can't remember a time that I'd been that close to him. He was big for his age. I was small for mine. Him being this close made me feel puny. Even though we had class together, I can't say I was ever this close to him.

"Yeah. Quinn."

"I thought so. I'm…

"Louis. I know. We had class together."

"You live in town?"

Of course! He was the invader here, after all. How had I been so invisible to him?

"Yeah. Up the hill."

"What're you reading?" he asked.

I showed him the cover and he said he hadn't picked that one up yet. We talked about comic books we've both read, and he told me about others I've never heard of.

"I'm exploring the town. Wanna ride around with me?"

"Sure." I rolled the comic and tucked it into the back pocket of my cargo shorts. I tightened the cap on my soda bottle and tucked it into the side pocket. And I straddled my bike and followed Louis onto the sidewalks and around the town.

We stopped in front of Mrs. Shealy's house. A bunch of little kids were out back playing hide-and-seek. It was late morning. I imagined she was inside cooking lunch for everyone. I used to stay at the daycare, but when my dad thought I was old enough, they stopped paying her to keep me over the summer and afterschool.

Louis watched everyone play.

"Bunch of little kids?"

"Yeah," I answered. "No one our age."

"So, what's there to do in this town?" he asked.

***

We continued riding the sidewalks. I led him to the empty baseball park. We rounded the bases as fast as we could kicking up a dust storm with our tires. Sufficiently dizzy, we made our way to the bleachers and parked the bikes.

"That was awesome."

"Yeah," Louis said.

"I haven't been on a baseball field in a couple years."

Louis sat up. "You don't play?"

It was standard for a southern boy to play baseball

or football or something. I, however, didn't. I hated the game. It was boring. I'd stand in the outfield chewing holes in my glove because people barely ever hit the ball out that far. And when they did, I couldn't field or throw. And batting was mostly me swinging at air. The entire game was embarrassing.

It was for my father, too. He made me play. He desperately wanted a normal son. When he came to the first few games, he seemed to almost cover his face in shame. After that, he never came to another game. But he still signed me up and made my mom bring me. It's like he wanted to continue my public humiliation as a sacrifice for his inadequacies. He so desperately wished that he was God that he bred his very own lamb to sacrifice.

"No," was all I said.

Louis shrugged it off and we laid on the bleachers for the next half hour watching the clouds pass overhead. They were shaped like dragons and mountains and knights and monsters. We pointed at them and concocted stories of epic battles across the heavens.

"You wanna come read some of my comics?" Louis asked after the clouds began looking like nothing more than cotton balls and marshmallows.

"Sure."

With that, we grabbed our bikes and walked them away from the baseball fields. "It's downhill all the way to my house. I'll race you!" And he was off.

I did my best to keep up, but his bike was so much newer than mine. And he was so much bigger. I could do little more than keep him in my sites as the wind blew my semi-long hair behind me. I felt so free.

By the time I reached Louis' house, he was already

at the door waiting for me. I dropped my bike and met him at the door. A massive dog barked from inside.

"Wait here a sec. I gotta get Pete or he'll run outside. He's a crazy dog."

Pete was a fluffy chow-mix pup. And he was friendly. Once we were inside, he jumped on me and started licking my face. Louis pulled him down

The house was a three bedroom. His parents had the larger room on one side of the house. The two others were his. He had a bedroom and a playroom. This kid had everything. There was Castle Grayskull and the Thunder Tank. Action figures galore. G.I. Joes. Transformers. Everything. I was in awe.

"They're in here."

Pete followed as Louis led me past the playroom to his bedroom. He had a full-sized bed and a TV. His bookshelf was lined with books and comics. Batman. Green Lantern. Dr. Strange. All the different X books. Teenage Mutant Ninja Turtles. He had so many I didn't know where to start. He tossed me a couple Justice League books.

"You should totally read these!" And that's exactly what I did. I kicked off my shoes, hopped on his bed, and opened the first comic. Louis sprawled out on the other side of the bed and Pete flopped down between us. And we spent the afternoon reading comic books until I looked over and saw the red digits on the clock on his bedside table.

2:43.

"Oh crap!" I jumped up and scrambled for my shoes. "I gotta go." My dad would be home shortly after three and he'd have me working until night. If I wasn't there, I'd be in it deep.

"You wanna hang out again tomorrow?"

"Heck yeah, I do."

With that, I was out the door, on my bike, and speeding down the sidewalk for home.

***

Louis was at my house the next morning only a few minutes after my dad left. He said he saw what house I went to and thought he'd go ahead and come over. I was glad he was there but told him to make sure not to come by while my dad's truck was in the drive. He didn't question me. He never did. Anything he ever learned about me, he learned because I offered it up.

I, however, quizzed him about everything. His family used to live up north. His mom was a realtor. His dad had retired from the army corps of engineers and took a job managing a major reorganization of the hatchery. They had moved around a lot. Louis was pretty sure that was why his parents kept him supplied with pretty much everything he asked for. He wasn't complaining.

We rode our bikes back to the park and hit the swings. There really wasn't much going on with the park. A few swing sets. Monkey bars. And a fifteen-foot metal slide that would scorch the flesh from your legs in the heat of the summer.

"What was the coolest house you ever lived in?" I asked him.

He stopped swinging and thought for a second. "I mean, they were all kinda lame, but I did once live in a haunted house."

"What?!"

"Well, my mom said she thought it was haunted. I never saw anything, but my mom swore things would move on their own."

"What kind of things?"

"Her keys. Stuff like that. My dad would tease her. He told her she just always forgot where she put them."

We laughed.

From there, the conversation focused on ghost stories. He told me about his grandma's house and how she said there was this ghost cat that would visit her in the night. When she would get up and follow this random cat out into the hallway, it would disappear through the door of an empty bedroom and be gone. She said it happened a few times. Louis said the funny thing was his grandma never had a cat. She had been highly allergic. But the ghost cat never even made her sneeze.

"That is crazy! Did the cat ever try to hurt her?"

"No. That's the weird thing. She said all it ever did was walk into that same bedroom. She said it must have been a message from my uncle George. He died when he was still a teenager and that had been his bedroom. My dad said she was most likely dreaming it all. There was never any sign of a cat or any other animal in my grandmother's house."

"There was this one time…" I started. But it felt silly. Like I was just trying to one-up him.

"What?"

"Back when I was younger, I stayed with Mrs. Shealy. I mean, until I was too old to be going to a daycare." I had to clarify before continuing. "There was this… witch's finger."

His face lit up and he stopped swinging.

***

I told him how we were playing hide and seek one day and a couple of us, me and the Derrick brothers ran out to this old barn she had way in her back yard. The Derricks were oddly blond boys with bright blue eyes and light blond eyebrows. They barely talked to anyone other than each other. We weren't supposed to go to the barn.

The old wooden door was chained but not too tight. We pulled it open enough and pushed through. The boards creaked and cracked as we climbed over the random stuff the old lady had stored out there. I had that spooky twinge in the deepest part of my belly. You know the one? When you just knew deep down that something was wrong… off.

The three of us ducked behind some old chests and tried not to giggle while we listened intently for the seeker. As time passed and my breath calmed down, it became obvious the hiding place was too good and we'd never be found. I looked around.

We were in a lower room. A ladder led to a loft where most of the floor had fallen through. The other side of the loosely boarded wall was a smaller storage area. It looked like more trunks and toolboxes in there. Lots of rusted things.

There was this one toolbox. Green, but most of the paint had flaked off exposing the rusting metal beneath. The top was open slightly and something stuck out of it. It was a fleshy dark gray finger with a sharp, black fingernail. And it hung limply from the top of this toolbox.

I made the Derricks come over. They saw it, too. I wasn't crazy. We had to get it.

I dug around and found one of those flex grabbers mechanics use to nab out-of-reach bolts and stuff. This old lady had all sorts of old tools and furniture stashed like she never got rid of anything. Even with the grabber, I couldn't reach the finger.

We heard Mrs. Shealy calling for us. It was lunchtime and no one could find us. We were going to get in so much trouble. The three of us ran to the barn wall and peered through. She was angrily calling our names. Not seeing us in the back yard, she walked around the other side of the house. That was our chance.

The Derricks pushed their way through the door. I had to have one more look. What I saw chilled my spine. The finger wasn't there anymore. The boys called and I followed them out. We ran for the house and were on the back porch when the old lady came back around and found us.

***

"When she asked where we'd been, we told her we were just hiding." I finished my story and Louis was in awe.

"Did you ever look for it again?"

Obviously, I had. Every chance I could while I was there, I ran to the barn and peered in searching. After I stopped going there, I still snuck over into the back yard when no one was around and tried finding it, but I never saw it again.

"We should go see if we can find it. See what else that old lady has hidden in there!"

The challenge was set. Louis was determined to unmask the witch or die trying. And I fed off his excitement.

We made our way to the back side of Mrs. Shealy's property, but all the kids were out playing. We couldn't get close without being seen. Louis said we should return later. He figured most of the kids were heading home by five and thought we could come back around six or seven when she's inside having dinner and we could have our run of the place.

I felt the blood drain from my face. My god no. This new freedom I found with Louis was fragile at best. How do I invite a very new friend… is that what he was… into the inescapable terror that filled my home?

"I… can't. I work for my dad in the afternoons."

"Oh. Well… we'll figure it out."

And that was it. He said he had to walk Pete and asked if I wanted to come. Absolutely I did. We saddled up and rode out.

"Look at this!" Louis shouted as he threw both hands in the air and guided his bike with his legs and hips. That was the most amazing thing I had seen in all my eleven years.

I tried.

Once. Quick. And I didn't crash. So again. Slightly longer. And no fall. So, I went all in.

I was flying.

My arms spread and I was a soaring eagle. I was the risen Christ. I was the pinnacle of human achievement. It was amazing.

Then the handlebars wobbled and I grabbed them tight. Terrified. My soul crashed back down into my earthbound husk. A freedom I had never felt destroyed out of terror. I became my own abuser.

Louis slid to a stop and laughed.

"Oh my god, that was so funny. Your face!"

I joined his laugh, but mine was peppered with gasps for breath. My heart throbbed in my throat.

"Are you okay?" he asked.

I gathered myself and nodded my head. I was good.

Pete spun circles of excitement when we grabbed the leash from the coat rack at the back door.

"He's really good on the leash," Louis said. He took the handle and wrapped it around his handlebars. "And he loves to run."

He did, too. That dog led us around town. He stuck to the sidewalks and only stopped to sniff and pee. Other than that, he smiled huge running ahead of us on our bikes. We bolted down the main road turning past the park. Blocks down and just past my house, we returned to the ball fields. Past the kids' full-contact football field to the cluster of little league baseball fields.

We dropped the bikes and led Pete onto one of the gated fields before closing the small dugout gate. Louis let Pete loose and that dog went apey. He ran from one edge of the outfield to the other. He lapped the field a handful of times and darted back and forth kicking up a cloud of dust. It was the funniest thing.

We tried chasing him, but there was no way we were keeping up. Still, we tried.

Louis and I collapsed somewhere between second and third base. We were laughing when Pete barreled into us. He was excited and wanted to play. We rolled him over and over until he finally gave out. Louis and I laid our heads on the panting dog and used him as a pillow while we gasped for breath in that orange haze created by ballpark dirt.

"Do you know Tonya Bradley?" Louis asked after our laughing had ended and our breath became manageable.

"Tonya? Yeah. She moved to town at the beginning of this school year."

"She cool?"

Cool? I didn't know what cool meant. I didn't know what she did with her time. All the kids in the class seemed to have been doing things together on the weekend, but I never seemed to know about it until after the fact.

"Yeah. I mean, sure, she's cool. She hangs out with the cool kids..."

"I mean, is she fun to hang out with? She invited me to her twelfth birthday party this weekend. She said that since mine is next week, we should have ours together."

"Oh. I didn't know it was her birthday." Of course, I didn't know. I was never part of the crowd who knew things like that. Or went to parties. Even if I could go, what sort of present could I take? A dozen eggs? Some squash? I mean, being allowed to go anywhere, or even having the courage to ask knowing it would be met with vitriol from a man who seemed to hate to be reminded that I was taking up space in his world, was as much a daydream as the ones I had that I'd show up and give the favorite gift and be accepted. So stupid.

"You should come!" Louis sat up quick which excited Pete again. He leaped up tossing me to the side. That dog was strong but dumb.

I climbed to my feet. "What?"

"If it's going to be my birthday party, too, you should come!"

Again, that crippling terror. Part of the daydream was coming true. I was being invited. But that meant I'd have to ask permission. I'd have to directly confront the man who treated me as if my every breath was the only gift I should ever expect from him and ask to be allowed to do something fun.

Work! That's it.

"Wow. That would be awesome! But I work around the house on Saturdays. I wouldn't be able to."

"Come on! I'm sure your parents would let you off the hook once. It's your best friend's birthday."

Best friend. I don't think I'd had one of those before then. I could walk across a bed of Legos and thumbtacks spread on the surface of the sun barefoot at that moment.

"Yeah. I'll ask." And that was it. He was thrilled. I was thrilled. And we needed to get Pete home.

Louis called him and he came running. Once he was on the leash, we left the field and grabbed our bikes. We pushed them to the sidewalk.

"Can I take him?" I asked.

Without hesitation, Louis tossed me the leash and I slipped it over my handlebars. We peddled forward remembering the downhill slope. We pushed the bikes faster and faster. It was awesome.

Until the cat darted across the road.

Pete turned immediately to the right. As is obvious, my handlebars went with him. Then the rest of the bike. My momentum, however, carried my body forward. I hit the roadside hard rolling through the rocks and across the asphalt. Parts of me tore. Other parts shredded. I still have a small piece of gravel under my skin in my elbow.

Louis slid to a stop and dropped his bike. He ran over and helped me up. He looked like he was about to freak out.

"Oh man, Quinn! Are you okay? You're bleeding everywhere!"

It hurt like hell, but I wasn't going to tell him that. "I'm fine," was my response. My shoes were scuffed up, my shorts splattered with blood, and my shirt torn. I knew I'd catch hell for that last one later. We're not made of money and all that. Maybe my dad would realize I had been torn to shreds before he smacked me for tearing up a good shirt.

All in all, my left knee and both my arms were scratched pretty good, and I'd busted my lip open. My toe hurt. When I took my shoe off at home later, I learned the toenail on my big toe on my left foot had been bent backwards. I'd lose it a week later.

"I'm so sorry. I didn't know Pete would- wait… Pete?" Louis realized his dog was gone and looked around. Pete had stopped at the other side of the road and was sniffing the ditch there. The cat must have disappeared into the storm drainpipe. Pete turned back to us with that big, idiot smile of the oblivious. He panted and drool dripped from his tongue evaporating on the road at his feet.

"Is your bike okay?" Louis asked helping me the rest of the way to my feet.

I looked to the scraped hunk of junk I called a bike. Picking it up, I pushed it forward and backward. Once I was satisfied that the wheels were straight, I hopped back on the seat. Louis smiled, grabbed Pete's leash, and got back on his bike. He'd be guiding Pete the rest of the way.

"Race ya," he said and watched me push forward before he started pedaling.

***

I got home with enough time to clean off my scrapes and change my clothes. I hid the shirt beneath my mattress.

My mom was home a couple of hours before my dad came in from the field. In that time, she made dinner and had it on the table just before he walked in the door. I never did figure out how she managed all that.

Dinner was quiet. My dad didn't care much for talking at the table. My focus was to be on eating. I wasn't allowed to leave the table until my plate was clean. My dad wouldn't leave the table until everyone was finished eating. That meant most nights I needed to be done before his massive plate was cleared. He didn't have the patience to wait for his ungrateful son to finish eating the food he worked so hard to put on the table.

Never mind that mom was the only one with a full-time job.

If I wasn't done before he was and if, like most nights, he was angry at the world, I was going to have hell to pay. So, when he came in, I was already at the table in front of my plate holding my fork. I was not going to give him an excuse. I was already hurting.

I wasn't but a few bites in when he stopped before sliding a fork-full of mashed potatoes into his mouth.

"Where have you been this week?"

I paused. Not long. I knew not to keep him waiting. "Just riding around. Going to the park and stuff."

"With who?"

"This kid from school. He lives up on the corner."

He slides the fork over his lips and scrapes away the potatoes. He partially swallows before continuing. "I need you around here more. Okra and squash needs to be picked."

I withered, but I didn't complain. "Yessir," is all I said and I ate.

I finished and sat at the table until he was done. He wiped his mouth, looked at my plate, and went back outside to finish up whatever he was doing.

I cleared the table without much of a word to my mom and took my bath. There really wasn't a reason to stay awake much longer, so I called it an early night.

My morning chores were done quickly and without hesitation. When my dad left for the convenience store, I was left with a blackhole where my summer had been. What was left were twenty or more pairs of dark brown, cloth work gloves and stacks of empty baskets.

I sighed and grabbed the first pair of gloves and a basket. If it didn't look like I'd put in a full day's work when he came home, he would use that thick, four inch wide leather belt on my backside.

Louis slid his bike to a stop no more than ten feet from me. "Wanna go to the park?"

"Can't." I motioned to the baskets.

"How much do you have to do?"

"All of it. Farmer's market is this weekend."

"That sucks."

The obviousness of his statement sent a pang of rage through me.

"Can I help?"

I had no clue how to respond. My friend would descend into hell at my side. He grabbed a basket and stepped up to follow me.

"You'll need gloves," I said.

"I'll be fine. I'm tough."

"Gloves," I repeated.

We went through five pair each by the time we broke for lunch. The spines shredded the fabric of each pair before a row was fully picked. But we had covered most of the field clipping the pods and filling basket after basket.

My hands were bloodied around the fingernails. Those things always tore me up. My dad said I should've been a girl with how dainty I was.

Louis's thick fingers looked dry and scratched, but he was fine. He said it must've been how he was twisting and snipping the pods. Still, his gloves fared no better than mine. He was just… Louis. I was jealous.

Lunch was peanut butter and honey sandwiches my mom made before she left for work. With a bit of milk, we turned on the TV and took our break in the living room. All I had was network, so the only things on were soap operas. But the early afternoon was hot, and we were bloated.

After lunch, we returned to the field and were working hard when my dad got home. I could see he wasn't expecting so much to be done.

He tried to suppress his admiration as he approached me. Louis stood a few rows away from me.

"Who's this?"

"Louis. My… my friend. From up the street."

He eyed Louis. It was as if he was looking at what he thought a son should be.

"Y'all did good today."

I was floored. A compliment was more rare than a deposit of painite.

He turned to Louis. "You guys did a solid day's work."

"It was fun," Louis called back.

"You want to keep it up?" He spoke to Louis but looked at me. "Three days a week. Ten dollars a day each. You guys get two days to ride around town? Interested? If it's okay with your parents."

Our shared excitement as we looked to each other for confirmation answered for us. Thirty bucks a week all summer plus two days to just goof off? The weekends were always family time with mom and church with grandma while dad worked, so two days during the week to just hang out with Louis was unbelievable. It was more money than I'd ever had.

"Heck yeah," he responded.

My dad looked at me. I nodded yes with a smile. The look on his face told me what I needed to know. This money was a gift. My freedom was a gift. No slip ups or it would all be gone. He would destroy me.

He left the field to change out of his work clothes – a black polo with an embroidered Shell logo on the chest and some khakis. Louis and I worked until after dark. We didn't finish the okra field, but we would in the morning. The squash was another day or so of work. We'd probably be done early with some extra free time this week. I knew we would be doing something else next week. There was always something to do.

I was starving by the time Louis headed home and I made my way in to wash up for dinner.

Dinner was the usual uncomfortable silence. I elected to not ask about the birthday party. I had just gotten everything I should have expected for that summer. How could I possibly ask for more?

After dinner, with him outside, I helped scrape the plate residue into the trash and put the dishes into the sink of hot, soapy water my mother had prepared. While she washed, I sat at the table.

"Mom?"

"What's up, baby?" I was getting too old to be called baby.

"You know Louis?" Of course, she did. She answered. My dad had told her already.

"His birthday is this weekend."

"We should get him something."

"There's this party." I told her everything I knew. She thought it would be fun. We would go Friday afternoon to the K-Mart and buy them both something. "But what about dad?" There was a hierarchy, and I was suddenly afraid of having this all go away.

"I'll tell him. It'll be fine," she said. "Go get your bath and brush your teeth." That was code for both the conversation being over and a command to end my evening.

I had no clue what to buy Tonya, but I knew exactly what I wanted to get for Louis. I knew he wanted a Stratos figure. Ultimately, because we were buying two presents on limited funds, I had to choose something cheaper than that specific Master of the Universe. I couldn't make up my mind, so my mother left me with the action figures to find something for Tonya.

I wracked my brain. Louis wanted that Stratos figure. How could I possibly show up with anything less. The G.I. Joe figures were cheaper. So were the crappy Hot Wheels. But I really wanted that action figure.

"What did you pick out," my mother said as she returned with some cheap shirt I was pretty sure Tonya would never wear.

"You're getting that?"

"I think it's cute. She'll like it," she answered.

"But that costs more than the Stratos," I protested. She looked at the price tag and then at the Stratos. I was wrong. The figure was two dollars more than the shirt. I could see her doing the math in her head. I saw her look at the shirt again. She was re-thinking getting it rather than splurging on the figure. "I have thirty dollars!" I chirped.

"You do?"

"I mean, not yet. But I will next week. I could pay you back."

She smiled. "Get it," she said and walked away.

I eagerly grabbed Stratos and followed my mother to pick out some wrapping paper and birthday cards. She picked out Tonya's card and I grabbed a Superman card for Louis.

The joint birthday party was at a skating rink one town over. More money. Plus, I couldn't skate. I promised more of my first paycheck to make sure my mom didn't back out. I knew we were spending way more than she initially thought. But she just smiled and tussled my hair and told me to have fun. She would be back in two hours to pick me up.

The decorations for the party were clearly for Tonya. Louis's name had been added to the pink and yellow birthday banner using blue stenciled letters. He didn't seem to mind.

When I got there, everyone was skating. Tonya and Louis's parents were preparing the snack area where they would have pizza and cake and ice cream. I was directed to deposit the gifts onto one of two tables: one for Tonya and one for Louis. Tonya's table easily had more than Louis's, but both were amazing hauls. I sat my gifts on the appropriate tables and walked to the half wall around the rink. Everyone seemed to be having such a good time.

Louis saw me from across the room. He was skating with Tonya and Barry and a few other kids from our class, but he broke away from them and cut straight through skating traffic stopping hard against the wall in front of me.

"Awesome! You came!" he said.

"I did."

"Go get your skates on and come out here." The other kids skated by calling to him to rejoin them.

"I can't really skate," I sheepishly answered.

"Go get skates. I'll teach you."

The skates were rented for everyone at the party, so I didn't have to worry about that. Once they were on my feet, I realized how terrifying standing on eight plastic wheels truly was.

I used the toe stops to tiptoe toward the oval concrete rink. Louis was waiting as I stepped onto the painted surface… and fell. He caught me and laughed as he went down with me. Once he was up, he helped me to my feet.

He held my elbow as we made two orbits around the rink. I struggled, but I only fell twice. I got good laughs from the other kids, but Louis helped me up each time and tried teaching me how to balance. By the end of the second lap, I was tenuously skating. Slowly. Carefully. But I didn't fall again. Louis tapped my shoulder or my head with a laugh each time he lapped me, but that did a lot to make me feel like I belonged despite the doubtful stares I received from my other classmates.

After the first hour skating, the parents called the kids to the concession area where they had finished decorating with balloons and ribbons and the birthday banner. Each seat was set with a paper plate and a single slice of cheese pizza and small plastic barrel of colorful flavored drink that I knew would taste amazing but for the odd chemical burn chaser in the back of my throat.

It was heaven.

Louis held a seat next to him when the kids ran to find theirs. The guys wanted to be near Louis. The girls clustered around Tonya.

"Quinn!"

The saved seat was for me.

We ate. We sang Happy Birthday to Tonya and Louis. They each had a cake and blew out their own candles. Cake. Ice cream. More sugar than the law should allow was pumped into our combustible little bodies. And we were exploding with energy once present time finally rolled around.

Tonya and Louis each received a gift to open. Tonya went first. Then Louis. That way everyone saw what each person got. It was weird and over-organized, but that was who Tonya's busy-body, stay-at-home mom was.

Tonya was first. I don't remember what all she got, but I remember being explicitly uninterested in almost everything.

Louis's first gift was a football helmet. I don't remember the team. But he loved it. He got a Megatron and Ecto-1. Everyone was going crazy. Then he got a Stratos. And he was elated. Only, the wrapping paper wasn't the paper my mother had bought. Barry had gotten him a Stratos, too. The next gift he opened was from me.

Another Stratos.

Barry laughed. It was a cruel one. He made some snide comment and the others laughed.

I felt small.

The only other time I had ever felt that small was standing beneath my dad's intimidating towering.

"This is awesome, Quinn!" He silenced the laughter with his excitement. "Now we have two to play with!" He then spoke to Barry, "You know, Stratos was the leader of Avion. This one can be Stratos." He held up the freshly unwrapped one. The one I gave him. "And this one can be one of his ministers of court!" I felt vindicated. Louis sounded beyond elated. I don't think he realized how amazing that made me feel.

"Oh my God, Tonya. What's that?" One of the girls hissed as Tonya pulled the shirt out of the box my mother had used.

"I don't…" She looked the cheap shirt over. Then she patronizingly looked my way. "Thanks, Quinn. I needed another bed shirt." She smiled. It felt fake.

***

The next few weeks were awesome. We were busy but managed to turn the work into games. Competitions. Louis won everything except when we had to move the animals between pens. He couldn't manage to get the pigs and goats to go where he needed them to. He almost fainted when we castrated the hog. Handling animals seemed to be my specialty.

Our free days were fat with comic books and sodas and candy bars and gum. We were rich and living it up. Louis' dad had an account with the video store, and he let us use it to rent some of the more tame horror flicks. Puppet Master and Jaws. I was in heaven.

Watching Tim Curry as It caught Louis. When George was dragged into that storm drain, Louis sat upright.

"We never found that witch's finger!"

No. We hadn't. I'd completely forgotten about it.

"We should go!"

"Now?"

It was a stupid question. Louis was already velcroing his shoes tight. Of course, he had those expensive shoes.

We were out the door and the wind was whipping past us in no time.

We took the long way around to the back side of Mrs. Shealy's property. It was early afternoon, and a lot of the folks were heading home for a quick lunch… at least those who lived close enough to work. We knew no one would really pay attention to two kids riding bikes in the heat of the afternoon, but we still ducked off the road and hid behind trees or in ditches. It just made it extra fun; like we were on a secret mission.

Detectives.

Spies.

Ghost hunters.

When we got to the back of the old lady's property, we laid our bikes on the ground just inside a few trees. No one driving by would see them.

The trees weren't thick. Mrs. Shealy could see the traffic going by from her back porch. But we felt covered as we crept toward the barn at the back of the property. She had the kids inside for naptime.

From the nearest tree, there was a good thirty-foot sprint to the back door of the barn. We looked to the house. The back door was closed.

"On three," Louis said. "One, two, three!"

We bolted from behind the tree and ran as fast as our legs could carry us keeping our eyes on the house for every step. We made the door, and I pulled it open just enough for Louis to slip through. I followed him and he pulled it closed behind us.

We peered through the wood slats of the barn. The door was still closed. We were safe.

Louis and I took a couple minutes to catch our breath. He seemed to settle down much faster than I could.

Once I was settled enough, he asked, "So, where is it?"

I smiled and led him to the back of the room. The tattered, old chair with the paisley upholstery she used to have in her living room had been tucked in there. Other than that, most of the stuff was exactly where it had been that day. Pointing through the boards, I identified the green toolbox.

"That's it?" He was mesmerized with the promise of a witch in that tiny box. "How could a witch fit in there?"

"I don't know. Maybe it was just her hand. Maybe there's some portal to a witch dimension in there and she was trying to pull herself through."

Louis's jaw dropped. "Holy cow! Think it could be?"

"I dunno. I just remember what I saw."

Louis looked around. "How do we get over there?"

"Used to be a ladder to get up there." I pointed up to a window above us that was the only opening in the wall. "I think the floor up there is rotten and Mrs. Shealy didn't want any of the kids going up there. The only other way is around."

I pointed to the front of the barn where there was another door. The door opened to an open covered space on the front of the barn facing the back of the old lady's house. She parked lawn mowers and rakes under half of it. The other half was a play area for the kids. There were two doors there. One opened to this side and the other opened to that one.

"We'd be seen out there," Louis replied. He looked back at the toolbox and pressed harder against the wall. The board bent a little. He let off and it returned to its original position. "The boards are warped. And old. I bet we could…"

He began working his fingers into the cracks on both sides of the aged slat. Once he had the tips through, he pressed and began pulling. The rusted nails creaked but held. He pulled his left hand out and pressed his right deeper into the crack to where he could get the first section of his three middle fingers bent. He put his right foot on the wall and pulled harder. I could hear the board cracking and the nails working free.

"Holy crap," I said.

"Help pull!" he ordered.

I grabbed around his waist and pulled.

The board snapped and we both fell back. I hit my

side on one of the trunks. Louis came down on top of me. My side was hot fire. My eyes were blurry with tears. I couldn't help but cry.

Louis cupped his hand over my mouth when the screen door at the back of the house screamed open. Mrs. Shealy stood on the porch as the door slapped shut behind her. She looked around the yard inspecting the barn and everything else she could see.

She adjusted her thick glasses after fully inspecting the yard and, satisfied, turned to go back into the house. But she didn't close the door.

Damn. Naptime must be over. I did my best to stop crying and to pinch the tears out of my eyes so I could see while Louis shushed me.

I tapped on the hand holding tight to my mouth and he loosened up enough for me to whisper, "We gotta go now."

He nodded and helped me to my feet. "Think we can make it?" he asked dusting me off.

"No." The kids were running out of the house and into the yard.

"Crap. Run!" Louis bolted from the barn. I was seconds behind him. Some of the closer kids were startled when we leapt out and ran for the trees.

"Who are you?" we heard some of them calling after us. But we just ran.

We swept up our bikes and pushed them fast up the ditch to the sidewalk.

"That way!" I yelled and pointed to our right. To the left was the convenience station where I knew my dad would be. Without question, Louis went right. We rode as fast as we could and didn't stop until we had gotten back to his house. We dropped our bikes and bolted across his porch, through the front door, and didn't stop until we collapsed on the floor of his room.

I winced when I hit the floor. It was hard to breathe through the pain.

"Holy crap! You hurt?"

"My side hurts."

"Let me see."

I pulled up my shirt and Louis inspected the darkening spot that would become a bruise by the next day. He sucked in air.

"That looks painful." When he touched it, I jerked back and punched his arm.

"Ow!" I screamed.

He laughed. "Sorry."

Just then, Pete leapt to his feet and angrily barked as he ran for the front door.

"Someone must be here!" Louis said and followed. "It's your dad!"

The pain disappeared and cold fire engulfed my torso. I pulled my shirt down and ran for the door. By the time I whipped it open, my dad had crossed the front yard and was stepping up onto Louis's porch. His truck was whipped carelessly into the short driveway. Then engine idled and the driver's side door hung open. I froze.

"What's this I hear about you breaking into Mrs. Shealy's barn?" he bellowed as he towered over me. "She called me at the store and told me you and some other boy she didn't know broke in and tore a hole in the wall." His meaty hand was in the air high above his head.

"It was my fault, Mr. Constance!" Louis's voice came from the open front door. My dad stopped in his tracks. He looked angrily at Louis. "I made Quinn go in there! I was curious." Louis looked down at me. It was the first time I saw terror on his face.

"You! You?" Synapses were misfiring between rage and the confusion of misdirected anger. He had shown something to an outsider. They were seeing him raw and angry in a way only those living with him had ever seen. "You can't just go on other people's property, Louis."

My dad lowered his hand and grabbed the back of my shirt collar. He dragged me from the porch and across to the passenger's seat. He opened the door, and I scrambled inside.

Louis had followed, but only to the edge of the porch. He held Pete's collar tightly. My dad rounded the front of the truck and pointed to Louis.

"I don't think we'll need any more help around the house, Louis. I'll let your dad know when he gets home." With that, he jumped behind the wheel, and he drove me home.

I was lucky that there were only about three weeks left in the summer break. I wasn't allowed to see Louis for the rest of the summer. Couldn't leave the house.

<u>Chapter2</u>

The first day of seventh grade was what I would imagine getting out of prison was like. I had been on lock down since that last day at Louis's. There wasn't a night that I didn't rush to bed just so I could fake being asleep before my dad came in from work. And he really didn't care to look at me, so I was allowed to hide in my room and save my chores for after he'd left the house each morning. The only part of the day we shared was the dinner table. And I trembled so much I was sick to my stomach before dinner was over.

But that first day, among the sea of kids filling the halls, I was able to breathe freely again.

I followed the sheet of paper I'd gotten at registration to my assigned locker number. I spun in the combination. I had to do it four times before I got it right.

The junior high hallways, seventh and eighth grade, were the newer wing of the high school, so mine was a practically new locker. It felt special having a private place, free of intrusion; a place where I would wind up storing a couple of books, folders, and discarded tests and never really using. It was simpler to just carry everything around on my back all day.

But that first day was special.

"Quinn!" My name cut through the cacophony of conversations surrounding me.

Louis was waiving toward me. I ran to catch up with him.

He told me about hanging out with Barry and Carmen and the twins. They'd apparently been hanging out over the last couple of weeks. He said most of us from homeroom last year were in homeroom together again.

Even then, there was a social order. The richer kids tended toward the honors classes and the others filtered toward the bottom. Only a few of us earned our rise above our stations.

But I was eleven. What did I know about anything then?

Louis walked me toward homeroom and said hello to all the popular kids along the way. I retreated inward refusing to make eye contact with anyone until I was safely in the classroom grabbing a desk next to Louis near the back.

We wound up with not too many classes together, though. Homeroom and Algebra were really it that year. Algebra was his only honors class.

We would mostly talk before school, at lunch, and then we would leave together. Algebra was also the last period of the day, so we walked to his house together. I'd have about a half hour after school each day before I needed to be home. So, I would walk to his house, and we'd play with his toys or read comics for twenty minutes before I would dart for home.

At least that's how August began.

By mid-September, Louis was lingering around school longer. He chatted with the other kids waiting to load onto the bus… the ones that lived out toward the lake.

That ate up most of our hangout time after school.

We still walked to his house together, but I didn't have time to stay. Most of the time. Sometimes, I had to leave before his other friends got on the bus.

The buses seemed to come earlier on Fridays in September. Louis and I were able to hang out again that first Friday.

"Hey. You wanna go to the football game tonight?"

"The what?"

"The high school game is a home game tonight. I was going to meet some of the other kids there," he said. "Are you going?"

I stammered. "I don't know. I- I'll have to ask." I shuddered at the thought of that. "If I can't, maybe I could come back and hang out," I offered.

"You ask your dad. If you can come, I'll see you there," he countered. Before my shoulders slumped a little too far, he continued, "Do you want me to come and help you ask?"

My eyes bulged. "No! I'm fine. I'll ask." We had been playing with the He-Man figures, but I was miles away. "I gotta go." I panicked. "I'll see you tonight."

With that, I grabbed my bookbag and bolted out the door. Once home, I unpacked my schoolbooks on the bed, took out my science workbook, and began filling out the questionnaires.

When my dad got home, he peeked into my room. "Homework? On a Friday?"

"Yessir," I lied.

"I figured you would want to go up to the big football game." My spine tingled. How did he know, I wondered? He must have seen it on my face. "Don't all the kids go to home games?"

"No," I said. Flashes of Louis hanging out with Barry and Chad and… Tonya… rapid-fired through my head. "Maybe a few of them, but I don't want to go."

Oh well was his final word and he went to change out of his work uniform.

When Monday came around, I told Louis I was sorry but I just couldn't go. He said it was a bummer. He said he wished I was there… that they had a blast. He said these things, but I think he saw through the lie.

"This Friday is a home game, too. Maybe he'll let you go if you tell him everyone will be there.

I said, "We'll see. I mean, it's just a football game. I didn't know you were into football."

"The game looks like a lot of fun, but we don't watch it that much. Most of the time, we're playing tag or hanging under the bleachers. We even got in a water fight after Barry spilled his water by accident onto Sheila." He laughed at that last bit as if he'd told the world's funniest joke.

"Sounds like a blast," I lied again. "I'll ask him when he's in a better mood."

I had no intention of asking. But the week wore on. Louis seemed like his old self even if he hung after school a little too long. We still talked about the latest Green Lantern issue. We still looked for each other in the cafeteria – even if the table was getting a little more crowded. The other kids seemed to be talking to me more. I thought that maybe there was a place for me in this popular group.

So, I asked. And I was allowed.

I told Louis, and he seemed thrilled. We'd meet at the gate at seven and go in together.

When I got to the stadium right before seven, however, Louis wasn't there. He wasn't there at seven. He wasn't there ten minutes after seven. Not twenty.

I stood there alone. Most everyone was already through the gate but for stragglers here and there. The pre-game show was about to start. And there was no Louis.

"Quinn?" His voice was behind me. On the other side of the fence. I turned around and saw him and the twins walking under the bleachers. "Hey man! Come on in!"

I was fuming as I paid my entry fee and passed through the gate.

"I thought we were meeting out there," I said. I tried to not sound angry.

"Oh yeah. Some of the others got here and were going on in. I figured you'd get here and just come in, too." One of the twins said something to Louis and they left him behind. "C'mon. We're over here."

I followed Louis to the other side of the tall, metal bleachers that made up the home side of the open-air stadium. There was a flat, grassy area on the other side where a game of tag football had started up. Everyone was over there including some highschoolers.

Louis re-joined the game. They had been playing for a while. He invited me to play, but I opted to sit on the side and just watch. Other than a couple of the prissier girls, all the kids, girls and guys alike, were playing football. The guys got a little too handsy. But everyone was having a great time.

Or, as in my case, faked it well enough.

Louis caught a pass and ran past the swarm closing in on him for yet another score. Apparently, the "new" kid was too fast for everyone.

After his touchdown, Louis ran over to me. "C'mon! We're a man shy on our team. If you play, we'll be even."

"I'm really not…"

"Cut the crap and come on!" Louis said while pulling me to the field of play.

Almost completely ignored by us all, the actual football game kicked off and the stands roared to life.

Our next play began, and I was ordered to go deep. Assuming that meant all the way down the field, that's where I ran. The pass lobbed high and was slow and still I managed to look like a ground handler directing a plane with orange flags as I leapt for and widely missed the football. A couple of obscenities were thrown about, but we re-grouped.

The older kid playing quarterback told me to not go out so far this time. I asked him how far and he looked at me as if I'd asked his dad's cup size. "Go deep!" he shouted as we dropped into formation.

Louis ran up behind me and spoke close to my ear, "Run out about halfway and then turn left."

I gave him a thumb's up the same time I heard "Dork" come from somewhere far behind me. I didn't know the voice and, when I looked around, saw my teammates glaring at me.

"Hike!" the quarterback yelled.

Not hearing it, I was met with a couple of shoves from kids as they ran forward. I darted down the field and cut across. When I looked back, the football was in the air and rocketing right for me. I reached for it but was clearly missing it. But I got to save face as someone on the opposing team barreled me down planting my face in the grass.

Louis was by my side instantly helping me up. I spit grass out of my mouth and wiped my runny nose as he helped me to my feet. Only it wasn't runny. It was gushing blood.

"Holy crap! Are you okay?" Louis called.

I looked around to see that I was the center of attention. There were some concerned looks. Some of the guys from both teams laughed. Then there was Louis standing there, helping me like a child.

"I'm fine!" I barked and pushed him away before running to the restroom.

Over the sink, I pinched my nose and leaned forward just like Shipwreck had told me to from the G.I. Joe PSAs. Blood trickled down my arm. By the time I released my pinch, the bleeding had stopped. I did my best to clean up in the copper-smelling water and dabbed dry with a few paper towels.

Once I was out of the restroom, I had a decision to make. Would I head home early and explain to my dad why I had wasted his money if I didn't want to watch the game, or would I rejoin the large group of people who clearly didn't care to have me around?

I opted to rejoin, but only partially.

I went back to the field of play but positioned myself on the grass closer to the actual game on the field pretending to watch. At one point, Louis called to me to come play, but I pretended not to hear. Instead, I hyper-focused on the real game trying to understand the plays and what each team was supposed to be doing.

At some point my fake-ignoring became real ignoring. The sound of the game behind me was drowned out by the cheering of the crowd watching the game in front of me. And, because I wasn't paying attention, I didn't realize the game behind me had ended.

As the marching band took the field at halftime, I turned around to look for Louis and found that the crowd of kids was gone. I was alone.

I began wandering as if I knew where I was going. As if I had a destination. But I found myself on the opposite side of the stadium before I realized where I was. I stopped and awkwardly turned back. Looking across the field, I saw Louis and the other kids joking and laughing around the concession stand. They had fries and drinks. And they were all enjoying themselves.

I slowly returned making sure that they would be gone by the time was back. They returned to the gaming field. I didn't. Instead, I climbed into the home team's bleachers and found an empty seat at the very top. I finished out the game there, and, as the crowd filed out, I made my way to the exit.

"Quinn!" Louis called. He was already outside the stadium fence and was talking to some of the other kids. "There you are! I thought you had left."

"No," I said. "I just lost track of you after everyone walked off."

"Oh. Yeah. We just grabbed some food at halftime. We're going to go out to the lake. You can ride along if you want."

"I can't." It wasn't really a lie. I knew I wouldn't be allowed to go. But it felt like a lie because the truth was that spending more time with those kids would be one of the worst kinds of hell. "I have to go home." I began to walk away but turned back, "I'll see you on Monday."

"Yeah, man," he said before running to catch up to the others.

***

That Monday morning came and went. I saw Louis, but he was always surrounded by others. Apparently, he and Tonya started going together out at the lake. She and her friends were hanging around him throughout homeroom.

Lunch was equally awkward. I went to the table where we normally ate together. While there were usually more people there than I was comfortable with, this day found the table filled. Louis didn't seem to notice as I walked by staring at him. I found the farthest seat away and had my lunch with my back to them.

When I crossed the road that afternoon, I looked back and saw Louis in the bus area talking with Tonya.

A week or so passed. I moved through the school days, my time away from the confines of home, moving drearily from one class to another as Louis lived the life of a rising star. I began having lunch alone sitting outside near the library. At first, I was miserable. There's an emptiness that comes when someone filling a huge portion of your life instantly becomes absent. But I grew to enjoy the alone time.

"Hey, man. Where've you been?"

The voice behind me startled me. I was engrossed in tucking my stuff away in my locker before heading for home when Louis seemed to materialize behind me.

52

"Sorry," he said. "Didn't mean to scare you." After I shrugged and closed my locker door, he continued. "You haven't been around at lunch for the last week. Everything okay?"

"Everything's fine. I've just been busy," I answered. I had found Alas Babylon in the library and was trying to get into it. This girl, Melissa, said I should try it. Melissa was in a lot of the honors classes I was and had become my conversation partner throughout the day. I started and stopped a couple of times before I finally hit chapter five. Then I was completely engrossed.

"Oh," he said. "Just hadn't heard from you in a while is all." He seemed uncomfortable.

"Yeah, well. All's good." I began walking away. The busses were the opposite direction and I saw the others through the doors waiting on him. He didn't follow me. When I looked back, he was walking through the opposite door.

I finished the book before the next week began. I hid a flashlight in my bed and read under the covers all night until I was finished. That Monday's lunch saw me back in the library looking for Melissa. She spent her lunches in there and I wanted another book suggestion.

Thanks to her, my first quarter of the year was filled with Stephen King and Tolkien and Ann Rand and H.P. Lovecraft. Some of these I couldn't find at the high school library, but she would check them out at the county library and let me borrow them. I brought my lunch into the school library and shared a table with her. We read and ate together every day.

Melissa was from the wealthier side of town. But she was homely enough to be left out. There was no place for people like us. Even though we were alone, we could be alone together. She had a pretty face, but the freckles and thick glasses mucked it up. And she was weird. One of those who didn't really care to act in a socially acceptable manner.

At the end of each day, she would hang near the library until her bus, one of the last ones to load, was almost completely boarded before running for the closing doors. She had the same desire to surround herself with the masses as I did. Rather than leaving immediately, I stood with her. We would talk about whatever we were reading that day.

By midterms, we had these conversations with fingers locked together.

At some point, we spent every free second possible together. Lunches. Walking from one class to another. Homeroom. And people took notice. Especially of her.

When Melissa joined the ranks of the girls in the class with boyfriends, she was allowed into their conversations. It didn't seem to matter that the boyfriend in question was me. She would hear the gossip. Get the beauty tips. We were never invited, but she would hear about the parties or the trips to drive go carts. How Tonya loved kissing Louis.

They asked Melissa if I had kissed her. She told me how they thought it was weird that I hadn't yet.

"To hell with them and what they think," I said.

It was another week before Louis cornered me in the bathroom. "Dude," he said. "Why haven't you kissed Melissa?"

"I… what? How do you…"

"Tonya. She says they think it's weird you haven't tried. And it totally is. Why?"

"I… I mean, she never said anything," I said.

Immediately, I realized I missed something big.

"Dude." Louis badgered me for a few more minutes before telling me to get it together.

The rest of that day, I was quiet. Focused. When I found her that afternoon, I was on a mission. As I approached, I wrapped her in our usual hug. But as we pulled away, I held. I moved in for a kiss. Lips puckered, I closed in. As my eyes were closing, she opened her mouth for a way different type of kiss. It was awkward as her open mouth closed around my puckered lips.

By the time I realized I had gone in for the wrong kiss, it was too late. I opened my mouth to meet hers. It was wet. Slick. Gross.

There were spaghetti noodles of slobber linking us as we pulled apart. I used the back of my sleeve to wipe it away. She did the same. We hung in the awkward silence for less than ten seconds before she kissed my cheek and said, "Bus!"

I watched her run for the bus and noticed, as I turned to leave for home, that there was still a line waiting to board.

There was no second kiss. By the end of the week, I had stammered through breaking up with her. She relieved me with, "Oh thank god!" And like that, the hand holding and book conversations were gone.

***

Over the next few weeks, Melissa sat with Tonya's click more. She seemed more comfortable with the in-crowd. No one brought up the kiss fiasco to me.

I say "to me" on purpose. I could tell they still talked about it. Giggled about it. The sideways glances and snickers at my back. I saw it all. Sure, I pretended to be oblivious, but I knew. The failed kiss was currency in the popularity market, and she cashed in first.

The worst part was when Louis, a few days into Melissa's social ascendency, stepped back from Tonya and her friends as they talked and laughed. The look of pity on his face disgusted me. It looked as if he was contemplating coming over and comforting me, but some of the guys called his name and he ran to catch up with them. If there had ever been a current of loyalty or friendship, this was the point when I knew… knew… the riverbed was dry, and those days were behind us.

In the separation, she got the friends. But I got the library.

With her finding lunch at what had become the popular kids' table, the library was free for me to explore. This is how I spent lunch for nearly the rest of my seventh-grade year. Nearly the rest because I didn't quite make it to the end of the school year.

Three weeks before the year ended, after most of the course work was done but for finals and after I had perfected solitude, I contracted mono. I had watched from a distance as friends came and went from Louis's inner circle. He and Tonya broke up at least twice. There was a fight between him and Barry that landed them both in detention for a week. I was completely invisible to the world around me. I doubt they noticed when I stopped coming to class.

Mono floored me.

The congestion built up in my chest. I wasn't recovering. Then I became extremely weak. Couldn't breathe.

I was gasping for air one night and my mom took me to the emergency room. Everything in my chest had solidified and built into pneumonia. I was in the hospital at the end of the school year. I missed finals. I missed the end of year parties. I missed yearbooks.

I missed missing all these things.

I was in and out of consciousness for the better part of that last week. I remember waking up once and I thought I heard Louis and my mom talking over the sound of the ventilator I was on. She was telling him that I couldn't have any visitors, but she would let me know he had come by. He was there with his parents. They exchanged "we'll be praying for him," platitudes before leaving.

There was a Baptist, a Methodist, and a Lutheran church peppered throughout our small town. The pastors for each dropped by several times. They all spent time with my mom outside. Apparently, I was so sick that God wasn't even allowed into my hospital room. As bad as things were, they were about to get worse.

Intercranial hypertension caused by ventilator-associated pneumonia is extremely rare. I won the lottery.

Pressure built up around my brain and I slipped into a coma. I was out for a week and a half as the doctors pumped me full of drugs and performed a series of lumbar punctures draining fluid from my spine.

I died.

Well, I died for six seconds. When I awoke again, the doctors had reduced the pressure on my brain and my chest was clear. Within a few more days, I was on my way home.

The summer was arriving just in time for me to be medically ineligible for outside chores. I spent the first part of summer recovering in my room. My dad was determined to make sure there would be no fun to replace the chores he was now required to do alone. I was expected to keep the house clean when I felt well enough to get out of bed. I was allowed to go to the library with my mom on the weekend, so I didn't mind.

I was a straight-A student when I got sick, so the principal offered to pass me. Doing that, though, was going to move me out of my honors classes for the first half of eighth grade. He said that if I scored high enough on my mid-terms, he could get me back into honors.

I counter-offered.

I would pass my finals over the summer. It took a few weeks because the district had to be involved, but I ultimately aced my classes and earned my honors seat back. Between Terry Brooks, Terry Pratchett, and Alan Moore, the rest of my summer was as close to bliss as I could get.

By the end of that summer, my parents were having more arguments than normal. Usually, most arguments were more my dad berating my mom over some pointless thing he found unacceptable. But the ones that summer were different. They were financial. Apparently, the hospital bills were rolling in and things were becoming very tight.

My dad got a second job. He sold most of the animals. My mom took on extra shifts at the hatchery and started classes at the technical school so she could be considered for future promotions. I barely saw them and the only times they saw each other were filled with arguing over money.

My eighth-grade year began with me begging pens and paper from my classmates.

The honors classes had most of the same players. Melissa. Tonya. The twins. But the classes were smaller.

Neither Barry nor Louis was in honors. I overheard Tonya saying they stopped trying last year. They had been going to most of the baseball games in the spring. Apparently, they were doing that instead of studying.

I was with most of the same people the first half of that first day. These were the classmates who were there when I got sick. The ones who finished last school year without me. And the warmest greeting I received was, "Glad you're feeling better." Melissa said that when I walked past her on my way to the back row of the class. No one else seemed to realize I ever returned to school.

Lunch rolled around and I hit up my locker. My papers and folders were still in there from last year. I decided to abandon the locker altogether.

"Quinn!" The voice was deeper than I remembered, but unmistakable. My name was accompanied by a heavy hand landing flat on my upper back resting there. "Glad to see you up and about," Louis said.

I turned to look at him and was forced to look up. The summer had been good to Louis. He was a couple inches taller than I remembered. His body had also filled out. His shoulders had broadened. His cheeks had become more defined. Beyond the early explosion of pre-teen puberty, Louis's muscles were far more swollen than they had been.

"Whoa," I said before catching myself. "You got bigger."

He chuckled. "Football will do that, I guess."

Football. I seethed. "You're playing football?" I think he could hear the disgust in my voice.

"Yeah. Barry and I went out for the JV team at the end of last year. I made quarterback!" he said proudly.

"Guess that's why I didn't see you around all summer." I turned and started for the cafeteria. He followed.

"I stopped by the hospital a couple times," he answered. "You were pretty bad off. Couldn't see anyone. Your mom let us know how you were doing. And she told us you were in summer school catching up."

"It wasn't summer school," I barked. "I made sure I stayed in honors."

"Ah," is all he mustered as a reply. Then, "Well, between you recovering and doing homework and never being out at the park… and practice of course… I guess we just didn't have a chance to catch up. But I'm glad you're better. That was scary."

"I guess," I said.

"You weren't scared?" he asked in amazement.

"I was asleep for most of it," I answered. "The worst part was having those tubes pulled out of my throat."

He was silent for a bit as I continued my trek across the courtyard toward the lunchroom. Still, he followed.

"Did you keep up with any comics this summer? Superman was pretty awesome."

"No, I haven't really read any comics for a while," I said. "Been sticking to real books. Besides, Superman is a little simple, don't you think?"

"What do you mean?"

"Every superpower in the world and all he does is fly around stopping freaks in costumes. Never makes any real change. Never does anything to stop crime before it happens.

Just seems like a waste of power to me." Louis stopped walking to think. I guess he couldn't manage to do the two things at the same time.

"That just seems… dark."

"Realistic," I answered. I opened the door to the cafeteria. "Are you going to lunch?" I asked when he stopped before following me inside.

"Free period. Was going to the weight room."

"Oh… yeah. Football," I spat.

"It's fun. I like it. I'm actually pretty good," he defended.

"Okay," I said turning to leave him behind.

"See you around?" he asked. We had a total of zero classes together this year. Our lunches were at different times. And he had practice after school.

"Sure," I lied.

He knew it was a lie. He answered with one of his own. "Cool. See ya."

I went about my lunch. He went to work out.

***

Louis was a god on the field; not that I ever saw him. The pep rallies were mandatory, so I got to see him in uniform. Tonya was a cheerleader. That meant that each pep rally turned into the junior high crowd cheering more for their flirting than the actual team. But, apparently, we won a lot. Everyone was excited.

We landed extra rallies thanks to Louis leading the junior-varsity to regionals, upper-state, and state finals. He didn't take the state title, but he was ranked. The local paper did a write-up on him. Everyone knew Louis Bryant.

It grew worse by baseball season. Apparently, the guy was a sports prodigy. Star quarterback. Better pitcher. He averaged three homeruns every game that season.

Not that I ever went to a game.

He was king of eighth grade thus king of junior high. He was hanging out with the older kids. Going to all the parties. He was already set to be in rotation for varsity quarterback. By the last quarter of the year, he was pitching and winning the State JV baseball championship while making every football practice.

I, however, had my own issues.

Classes came easy. I didn't have to study much to maintain my nearly perfect grades. Any romantic prospects would never materialize thanks to the kissing fiasco the year before. I resigned myself to the solitude of the library when I wasn't in class. My unthreatening, and forced, asexuality made me perfect as the class's tutor. Twice a week, Melissa, Rebecca, and… what was her name? I don't remember. But twice a week they would come to the library, and we'd work through algebra.

That didn't sit well with Sid Chase.

Sid was another poor kid that lived in the town proper. He was so far on the other side of town that our paths never really crossed. I wasn't sure how he managed to get into the honors classes, but he was struggling. He was also in that group of kids who would leave campus right after school and smoke before boarding the busses. Teachers and administration didn't' lift a finger against them so long as it was off campus.

He was also one of those funny-smelling kids. I know there was a stink to my home, but my mom worked hard to keep us in clean laundry and to make sure I bathed daily. Her early years were filled with outhouses and beehives and six kids in a one-bedroom house. We were clean.

Oh, and Sid hated me. He had been my only fight in elementary school. He was a big fan of professional wrestling. One random day on the playground, Sid decided a clothesline was in order. I remember the back of my head hitting the ground and I remember him standing over me laughing. But I don't remember the time between that pain and my fists pounding his face while he flailed madly under me. I had his arms pinned with my knees and I was beating the living hell out of him.

We spent a week's worth of lunches in the principal's office after a solid paddling. They still did that abhorrent crap. My mom was livid. That principal had been the one to ask her about the belt-shaped welts on the back of my legs and here she was striking me without permission.

My seventh-grade year was spent blissfully Sid-free. But he was back in honors in eighth. He liked tripping me when I walked by. He got laughs when he pegged me in the back of my head with a spit ball. I tolerated it the first half of the year. But the second half started with me taking action.

I pulled Sid aside and said, "You need to back off. You don't like me. I don't like you either. We can live with that. But I'm done taking your crap. Stay away from me."

He tried to puff out his chest and seem menacing, but I had been experiencing my own little growth spurt throughout the year. I was taller than him by a few inches. "Or what," he grunted.

"I don't have to fight you to beat you, Sid." My eyes locked with his. I snarled his name as if to punctuate my resolve. He looked away. My heart raced. My legs burned as if I had just run a mile. We locked wills and I won.

We had placed our bookbags in our next class before leaving for our mid-morning break when Sid checked me into the lockers. He pushed hard against my head slamming it against someone's steel combination lock. "You're dead." He was inches from my ear and growling so no one else could hear.

And with that, he was gone. He joined the throngs in the courtyard for a few minutes of sun between classes. The heat in my legs had returned with the adrenaline surge. But it was a trembling heat that weakened my knees threatening to topple me to the floor.

Instead, I went back into the classroom.

With break, I had the room to myself. I paced and I cursed. I was both terrified and furious. I was facing the reality that a serious beating was heading my way… either at lunch or after school. While I was taller than Sid, I was a toothpick, and he was thick.

Two kids came in early from break. I can't recall who they were, but they caught my eye as they entered. Beyond them, Mrs. Steele was watching the hall making sure everyone was returning to class.

I didn't hesitate.

"Hey!" I called interrupting the kids' conversation and getting their attention. "Wanna see something cool?" When you read a lot, you get a head full of random trivia. Things like the loopholes kids like Sid used to hide their cigarettes in their bookbags leveraging the school's inability to search kids' bags without proof or actual threats of danger.

This, of course, helped troublemakers like Sid. They easily kept their tobacco safely hidden on them.

Unless someone like me intervened.

With the two early arrivals sufficiently interested, I grabbed Sid's bookbag and pulled his pack of cigarettes out. They looked at me as if I were an idiot and walked away. Mrs. Steele, however, did her job.

"Excuse me," she called as she approached. "Whose are those? Whose bag is that?"

I disclosed all. Sid was scooped up and taken to the principal's office before class began. He didn't return that day.

Or the next.

The rest of the week passed before the rumor mill funneled the information to me. Sid was on indefinite suspension pending and expulsion hearing. With the cigarettes, they were able to search his bag. They found a knife... one of those folding, serrated blade knives with a three-inch, black steel blade. Flea market treasure. And they found a zippo. He most likely carried it for his cigarettes, but lighters were banned, too.

I felt vindicated. I knew he'd have taken that knife to me when he came for me.

Sid was expelled the next Monday.

***

A few weeks later, I slid into my old rhythm. Class. Lunch. Class. Home. Repeat. The eight-grade jocks congregated in the front of the school. Most of them got daily rides home from high school jocks. No more slumming with the masses for the popular kids.

Rather than parting the sea of meat to go home, I took the long way around the library and exited the campus at the top of the hill. It was a longer walk home, but I would rather that than weathering the tsunami of taunts from the athletic click. The worst part was seeing Louis out there doing nothing about the teasing.

The new route took me closer to Sid's friends smoking circle. They eyed me but said nothing. I could handle the leers. They were easy to ignore.

One Thursday, things changed. The smokers saw me and moved toward me. I continued walking and looked down. They were probably going to the busses. I convinced myself I was just later than usual. I almost believed it until they stepped in front of me blocking my path.

"What?" That's all I got out before someone grabbed the handle on the top of my bookbag and pulled me. I lost my balance and was slung into the side of the brick building hitting my face. My mouth tasted like pennies. I spit blood when I was punched in the side.

Sid's friends surrounded me as I was pinned against the wall… by Sid.

He punched me in the stomach. I doubled over, but he quickly pushed me back upright. He pulled something out of his pocket and held it out so I could see the sun shimmer against it. He pressed the button in the handle and the switch blade appeared.

I heard him say, "…kill you." I heard him call me names. I saw hate in his eyes. I saw him push the blade toward my side. And then I saw the back of Louis's head.

He had stepped between us and wrapped his arm around Sid's arm keeping the knife from hitting either of us. I heard Sid yell before he dropped the knife. Louis hit him. Hard. Sid hit the ground, scrambled to his feet, and ran. His friends followed.

Louis turned to me. "Are you okay?"

His face betrayed his pity for me. I was humiliated. Emasculated. Made impotent and lesser-than.

"I'm fine," I said. "Thanks," I growled. And I walked away.

Louis rode into the end of the school year an all-American hero. Male beauty contest winner. Junior-High homecoming king. He did everything.

Everything, that is, but studying.

There was a rumor that he was supposed to fail eighth grade, but the coach stepped in. Secret extra credit or something. He couldn't play if he repeated the grade. They wanted him to play.

Without earning it, Louis followed me into ninth grade.

Chapter 3

Ninth grade began just like junior high. I walked to and from school. Stuck to myself. Hyper-focused on classes and grades. My dad had stayed off my back the last couple of summers thanks to the hospitalization. But that started to change when I went into high school.

He fought more with my mom. Nearly every night, he found something wrong with dinner or how clean the house was. How she tolerated his crap for so long, I'll never know. She had just gotten a promotion to shift manager and it came with a couple extra bucks per hour. She was finally pulling in more money than he was.

Though, that wasn't very hard. He had been spending more time away and the farm was falling into disrepair. The tractor blew a gasket and needed serious repairs… repairs he couldn't afford. Weeds were choking out the fields. The barn was suffering from years of neglect. And he was spending more and more time at the convenience store outside of his shifts. Things were spiraling. He grew more and more angry.

It was obvious he hated being home.

The old man had developed gout in his knee. He leveraged that every chance he got. Need groceries? Gout was acting up and he couldn't drive. Grass needed cutting? Not possible. Pipe burst under the kitchen sink? Screw it.

My mom and I did what we could to keep everything functional while my dad was phoning in his presence... unless he was screaming at her. I knew it was money-driven. Even at thirteen, I knew we were in trouble.

Before winter break, there was a special event at the school for the honors kids. Our school was launching a few new advanced placement, college-credit courses. I was one of the twelve kids selected to move onto the college track. That meant my schedule the next half was going to be intense. They wanted it to be a monumental announcement, so the school put on an exclusive banquet where they gave the selected students a plaque.

My mom was excited. We dressed in our Sunday best and went to the school.

My dad sat it out.

When we got home, he was sitting in his recliner flipping channels.

"Look," my mom said to him holding the plaque up for my dad to see. It was engraved black metal plated onto a dark wood background. "AP Eligible," it said. Had the school's mascot at the top. "Quinn is going to be taking college-level classes." I could hear the pride in her voice. Of the two of them, my dad was the only one who had gone to college. He didn't finish, but he'd gone.

"And?" He was unimpressed.

"And, you could be proud of him," she answered and handed me the plaque.

"What good is that?" There was a slur to his voice. I had never seen him so much as touch a drink, but there was a looseness to his drawl that betrayed his buzz. "It's not like we can afford college."

Cold chilled my spine again. He was stomping on my hope as quickly as I had felt it. My skin prickled all over as if billions of microscopic needles were fighting to erupt from every pore.

"You never know. They have scholarships out there. He's smart." She answered. I could see her in my peripheral vision trying to lock gazes with me as if she could will me free of the emotional destruction taking place.

I wouldn't look at her. I stared at him. I wished I could telepathically stop his already-dead heart.

Lightening fast, he flicked the lever on the side of his recliner and was on his feet and across the room snatching the plaque out of my hand. He raised it over his head threatening to swat me with it. "He ain't going to college!" he shouted.

I cowered.

My mom shoved him. He lost his balance and fell against the wall dropping the plaque at my feet. But he was up and on her in an instant. His meaty hand gripped her neck as he slammed her against the far wall while rapid-firing curses in her face.

"Stop!" I yelled. But he didn't. I grabbed at his arm trying to pull him away, but I'd sooner have shoved a bull. He elbowed me back and continued screaming how worthless she was and how she was the worst thing to happen to him. Her face was moving from red to purple. I just knew he was going to kill her.

Without thinking, I brought my heel down onto the side of his gout-riddled knee. He screamed and released my mom dropping to the floor cradling his knee. My mom gasped for air until the color mostly normalized on her face.

"Go!" She ushered me out of the living room, through the kitchen, and out of the house. She shoved me into the car and then slid behind the wheel.

We spent that night on the recliner and couch of my grandmother's one-room apartment in the independent living community she had moved to a few years prior. We bought a few days' worth of clothes at the thrift store in town, and, that Monday, my mom left me with my grandmother and returned to the house when my dad would have been at work. She returned with all our clothes, bedding and a few other things. By the end of Christmas break, the two of us were living in a twenty-year-old single wide in the trailer park on the edge of town.

My dad never came for us. Within a month, he had moved in this girl who wasn't more than two years out of high school. By the spring, the farm had been seized by the bank and he moved out of town.

The walk from the trailer park was longer than where we used to live. The wood laminate was peeling off the counters. The air conditioner barely worked. And, the hot water heater had fallen through the closet floor of the master bedroom and stood, instead, on cinderblocks. But the freedom I felt, the weight lifted from my shoulders, was more than I felt I ever deserved.

When the spring rolled around, I got a job at the feed mill at the far side of town. It was an under-the-table cash job, but the owners knew my parents and they knew what had happened so the job was a favor to help us stay afloat in our new life. I would walk to school and then to the feed mill where I loaded bags of feed into vehicles and help grind grain for livestock for the area's farmers. My mom was off work about the time the mill closed, so she would drive me home.

***

High school was a bit of a blur after that. My trajectory was set. Tons of honors and AP courses. College credit. Loads of library time. I was on a first-name basis with Elenore Smythe, the octogenarian who spend her waning years tending a mostly empty school library.

I managed a free period most semesters that I dedicated to pouring through every book on the shelves. It was the early nineties, and I was surprised at a few of the books I found. There was a solid selection of Toni Morrison, Octavia Butler, and Stephen King. Of course, we read Harper Lee and Mark Twain in class. It seems that while the book burners and "child protectors" were busy getting books removed from the shelves at larger schools around the state, my high school went largely overlooked. I made it my mission my sophomore year to consume every banned book I could find. When I couldn't find it, Elenore took fewer than two weeks to get it approved and added to her shelves.

"What're they going to do to me, Quinn? Fire me?" she would ask every time I feigned surprise when she handed me books like Pomeroy's Boys and Sex. "I'm eighty-two," she added before chuckling and walking away. Librarians truly are the warriors of the People.

While my junior high lunches were spent in solitude, there was a growing clique of outcasts congregating around the library in high school. Some of those joining the throngs were from my grade. They spent their first couple of years enjoying lunch in the temperature-controlled cafeteria, but the older populars seized total control of lunchroom seating by the time ninth grade rolled around. With nowhere else to go, they began to cluster in the covered walkways of

72

the library courtyard. There were older outcasts there, too.
Everyone ate and read and skateboarded and left the others
to themselves. We were a grazing herd of the unwanted and
ignored.

We also happened to be some of the smarter kids in
the school.

Don't get me wrong. There were plenty of the trendy
kids in the honors classes. But you haven't lived until you
listened to Alison Rhodes and Yvonne Johnston completely
map out Anne Rice's novels. They were better than a
conspiracist's corkboard when they connected every vampire
Rice chronicled through their siring all the way back to
Akasha and ancient Egypt. And there wasn't a soul who
wouldn't gather around when they were daydreaming about
The Claiming of Sleeping Beauty. Puberty forced everyone
to drool over the erotic landscape painted by the goth girls.

And there wasn't a page of A People's History
of the United States that Gene Ray couldn't recite as he
ranted against the encroaching influence of the thousands
of churches over our State Legislature or the erasure of the
evils of colonialism and capitalism through public school
indoctrination. He may have been a bit unhinged, but the guy
was entertaining.

They all had vast amounts of knowledge of the most
random topics. I remained a sponge on the periphery soaking
up every rant and adding their books to my to-be-read pile.

Late in my freshman year, Gene Ray and Alison
started dating. I can't say either were what I could consider
attractive, but their romance was one for the history books.
They barely sat together at school but lived next door to
one another. Rumors flew for the more than three years they
dated that they had slept together. But Gene would never
confirm, and Alison vehemently denied every claim. Their

PDA was non-existent.

They were more like two best friends who just happened to be dating. In fact, their relationship was most obvious when they fought. Their fights were epic. Alison had a solid right and Gene Ray loved flipping benches in anger. They always made up. Things were generally fine by the end of the school day as the last bell rang and the outcasts clustered just off campus to smoke.

That is, until things were no longer fine.

Gene Ray was a year ahead of me in ninth grade. By the time my senior year rolled around, he was still a junior. Alison had been, and remained, in my grade. I think the reality of her graduation approaching with Gene Ray increasingly apathetic about school was a stressor for her. Not to mention, Gene Ray turned eighteen that year and all he could talk about was dropping out. Alison had college on the brain. Things didn't fit well anymore, and she dumped him. Gene Ray spiraled after that. Drinking. Drugs. Two weeks before his eighteenth, he rolled his eighty-four Chevy Monte-Carlo through the huge peach orchard outside town taking out nine trees before coming to a stop.

He was in intensive care for about two months before his parents pulled the plug. There was a memorial assembly in the gym that seemed more pep rally than Gene Ray-focused. Student government was infected with popular kids, and they were responsible for the assembly. Not one of them cared to know Gene Ray. There were pictures of him printed and taped to the walls. Flowers from the local church. Pastor Spokes from Gene Ray's parents' church was invited to speak. He delivered a generically moving sermon for those who knew nothing about the avid atheist, but those of us who were Gene Ray's friends skipped out when the jocks followed the pastor to the podium dedicating that weekend's basketball game to his memory.

The whole thing was grotesque. Complete showmanship. Mindless. Heartless.

Alison skipped the memorial. When the group of us bailed early, we found her sitting alone under a dogwood tree in the courtyard where she and Gene Ray spent most of their lunches. It had been planted years ago next to the new library and a time capsule was said to have been buried there. They wouldn't be opening that for another ninety years. There was a weird little plaque in the grass marking the location. The plaque had been her throne… the goth queen and her skinny, metalhead king.

Her eyes were thick with cried tears. Her pasty makeup smeared when she wiped them away as we approached.

Yvonne slid onto the grass next to her and wrapped her arm around Alison's shoulders. "You okay?" she asked.

She choked unable to form a word and simply nodded. After swallowing, she asked, "Was it as bad as I said it would be?"

"Worse," Yvonne answered.

We spent the next twenty minutes raging on the student council and the administration for how they refused to let any of Gene Ray's friends speak at the assembly. In fact, I was the only one asked, but after the school shunned Alison and the rest of the group, I declined.

I had been asked because I was on the track for valedictorian, and they thought I would best represent Gene Ray's friends. Accepting the gig, however, felt like a betrayal. We were the life blood of the school We were the ones who published the newspaper and assembled the yearbooks. While the vapid masses moved through their days gossiping over the most recent hook ups, parties, and sports, we organized petitions to bring options to the cafeteria.

I found out later that day that Louis had spoken at Gene Ray's memorial.

By the end of the ninth grade, Louis had reached god status. He had taken the starting quarterback spot early in the season and kept it throughout high school. There wasn't a year we didn't go to state. And we lost state only once. That was the year Louis' dad died and he missed the big game.

He was everything anyone would talk about. Football season. Baseball season. All around amazing guy. His grades were crap, but he was coasting through. There was no way any teacher would stand in the way of the tickets he sold out game after game. There were features in the local paper every year. Yvonne even did this full issue feature on him in the school paper. Scouts from nearly a hundred colleges around the country came out to watch him play.

I even made it out to a game.

It was my junior year and I had a huge crush on Charlotte Pierce. Charlotte had come to live with her cousin Richard Wright, an awkwardly tall and thin guy with a pencil-line mustache clinging to his top lip. Richard was part of the anti-clique, clique, so Charlotte began her time at our school hanging out with our group.

She didn't stay in town long. Her dad was working in the Alfred P. Murrah Federal Building in Oklahoma City when it was bombed. A few weeks after that, Charlotte moved home to be with her mom.

Charlotte was a pretty girl. Like, model pretty. Long legs. High cheek bones. Tight, curly hair that fell halfway down her back. She didn't notice that every straight guy and lesbian in the school nearly broke their necks every time she walked by. I had my own share of double takes.

She wasn't an outcast. As such, she quickly lost interest lunching with Richard's crew. She found her way to acceptance by the popular kids and moved her lunches into the cafeteria with them. And Louis.

She only had eyes for Louis. Louis, however, had eyes for every pretty girl in the school. He and Tonya had broken up for the last time early sophomore year and he had his pick of the school. And pick he did. It seemed he had a new girlfriend every month. And Charlotte wanted her place in the queue.

One Friday, Richard mentioned he was having to go to the home game because Charlotte had convinced his parents to take her. It was the big event every Friday night in the fall, so it wasn't hard for her to convince them. But they weren't going to let Richard stay home. He had been caught kicking over trashcans behind the FFA greenhouse and had after school detention. They had him on a short leash.

"I'll come!" I chirped a little too enthusiastically. "So, you don't have to suffer that alone."

Richard shrugged and said, "Cool." And, just like that, I suckered myself into a football game. I hadn't been to one since going years before, and I very nearly regretted offering. Reminding myself that Charlotte was going to be there bolstered my will.

I found Richard sitting in the stands with his parents. Charlotte was nowhere to be seen. When I asked where she was, he answered, "She went to sit with some friends or something." And, just like that, my night was shot.

The pre-game show was filled with tribalistic fervor as the band and the cheerleaders took the field and the mascot danced around. Smoke bombs and a cannon had been added since the last time I went. The boom shook the stadium and the crowd erupted as the fight song blared from the field and the team took center stage. They tore through a giant, paper curtain painted with the opposing team's mascot comically trounced by ours. Professional wrestling was increasingly popular, and this had all the pomp of the biggest spectacle matches.

Leading the charge through the paper barricade was Louis, hero quarterback and local celebrity. He whipped his fists through the air and the crowd responded with louder and louder cheers. This was a teenager having his grotesque ego coaxed by frothing adult fanatics. I groaned to myself.

After the band and cheerleaders cleared the field, representatives from each team met around the head referee. We won the coin toss and elected to receive. Renewed howls and cheers from the crowd roared.

"Do you want to wander around?" I asked Richard as the teams took the field.

"Nah. Let's watch the first bit at least."

I looked to where the clearing used to be where the kids would play their own game of tag football. It was gone. Instead, new stands had been constructed. Every seat was filled. A winning team could really pack the home games. No wonder the paper and the debate club had received no additional funding over the previous few years and classes were using eight-year-old textbooks, I thought. Everything the school had was being funneled into the sports cash cow.

Kickoff was followed by yet another burst of cheers. Our team caught it and immediately knelt about three yards from the opposing end zone.

"Why wouldn't they try running it back?" I asked Richard.

He pointed to the field as Louis popped his helmet on and ran out. "Gotta give the star quarterback enough room to work."

The teams lined up and Louis shouted plays. The ball was hiked, and the flurry of activity began. He fell back into the end zone and watched as receivers ran deep. One of the opposing players broke the line and charged him. Louis held the ball high in one hand and, with his other, wrapped his arm around the charging player and spun slinging the guy to the ground. He finished his spin and threw the ball.

It spiraled halfway down the field and hit the receiver hard in the chest. The guy managed to close his arms around the ball just in time to be tackled. More cheering.

"Number eighteen, Barry Dennis receiving. First and ten on the forty-nine-yard line," the voice over the stadium speakers called.

Louis shouted line up commands to the team as they ran down the field barely giving the opposing team time to regroup. Louis handed the ball off this time and the runner was almost immediately brought down.

"Second and nine mid-field."

The third play looked like another pass set up, but all the receivers were covered. Before three tacklers could rush him, he ran.

He leapt as two would-be tacklers collided with two blockers and all four collapsed to the ground. He cleared them in a single vault and continued his run. No one behind him seemed to be able to catch up. One guy broke off guarding a receiver and ran at him jumping and wrapping his arms around Louis's waist. Louis dragged the guy at least five more steps before he slid down far enough to tangle Louis's legs and drop him.

"First down and goal!" the announcer shouted. "Louis Bryant gains forty-seven yards."

I could barely hear the speakers over the crowd. I felt my heart drumming in my ears and noticed my jaw had fallen open. I'd never seen such a thing. At some point, I had joined the crowd on my feet.

Within four plays, we had our first touchdown.

And so it went. The opposing team was good. They managed thirty-seven points against our eighty-four. Somewhere along the way I became as engrossed in Louis's performance as everyone else. I only left my seat during halftime to grab some food.

I saw Charlotte from afar after the game. She and her cadre of popular girls had gotten out onto the field and were talking to the team. She was smiling big and talking to Louis.

I watched the two of them flirt when Richard asked his parents, "Do you want me to go get her?"

"No," his dad said. "She's going out to the lake with those kids." Then they said their goodbyes and left me alone watching my hopes dry up and blow away.

***

I arrived early that next Monday morning. I had an experiment due in AP Chemistry that Friday and needed to set up the final stage before classes started.

When I was finished in the Chem lab, I walked into a hall flooded with students. There seemed to be a new excitement in the air. Everyone was clustered with friends and excitedly prattling on about some nonsense or another.

When the doors opened and Louis entered, however, the throngs of conversations ended, and cheers and applause filled the hall. Louis seemed humbled as he looked to the floor and made his way to his locker. Kids clapped him on his back as he passed. Someone started chanting his name and everyone else joined in.

He turned from his locker and put his hands in the air until everyone grew quiet. "Thanks, everyone. Can we please have a normal day?"

Someone shouted, "Superman wants a normal day!" Laughter filled the hall. Louis shook his head and moved on.

I saw Charlotte and Richard standing not too far away and walked over to them.

"All that for a football game?" I asked.

"You didn't hear?" Richard asked.

"Hear what?"

"Louis saved a mom and her kid Friday night," Charlotte added incredulously.

I hadn't heard that.

"We were all headed out to the lake," She began. "There were at least ten or twelve cars. The whole team. All the cheerleaders. A bunch of us. Apparently, they gather at boat dock six to celebrate every week.

"We were having fun. A bunch of us were skinny dipping. Louis sat on one of the picnic tables with Barry and a few others. He wasn't drinking or anything, but he seemed to be having fun.

"There was some argument between Jordan and his girlfriend. I don't remember her name. She goes to another school, and I'd never met her before. He had been drinking and she tried to take his keys, but he wasn't having it.

"Louis moved to calm him down, but Jordan jumped into his car and peeled out throwing rocks and everything at his girlfriend and a few others. He tore onto the road and barely had control as he pulled onto the small bridge. Another car was coming. Jordan crossed the line and clipped the back side of it. It spun and broke through the concrete rails seesawing on the edge.

"Jordan stopped and looked back before speeding away.

"Before anyone else had a chance to react, Louis ran up the hill to the bridge with Barry right behind him. The car engine rattled, and there was a fire under the hood. Louis grabbed the teetering car under the back tire well and pulled the back end to the road. He told Barry to sit on the trunk so it wouldn't fall and then looked in.

"There was a little girl in the back seat. Maybe five or six. Her Mom was unconscious in the front seat. The doors were jammed, and he couldn't get them open. So, he just started punching the window.

"He broke the back window and got the girl out but couldn't get the mom. So, he just started pulling on her door. I mean, he strained.

"The rest of us got to the bridge as the fire under the hood grew. It wasn't going to be long before the car was engulfed. Tonya took the girl back down the hill to get her away. Louis shouted to everyone else to stay back and he pulled on the door some more.

"It finally broke free, and he reached in pulling the woman out slinging her over his shoulder. He shouted to Barry, and they ran from the car. The fire was everywhere when the car finally slid off the bridge.

"It was unlike anything I'd ever seen. We stayed until the ambulances arrived and the cops had a chance to interrogate everyone. They arrested Jordan Saturday morning." She paused as I took it all in. Then she added, "But Louis is a legit hero."

***

Our high school careers ended the way they began… me working hard for what came easily for Louis. He was popular. Athletic. Attractive. Envied by his peers and adults alike.

I was… not.

But I did have some things Louis never had. I had a unique intellect that kept me at the top of every class but for P.E. I also possessed the drive that comes from a complete lack of privilege. When your every day is filled with suffocating greatness, rising above was the only way to breathe.

I excelled.

Still, Louis's shadow was dark and cold. Graduation was upon us, and a completely new predicament befell our school administration. I was leaps and bounds beyond my peers and was named valedictorian. However, student government demanded Louis speak at graduation instead. Their reasoning was that our class had a unique opportunity to have a "hero" speak as class spokesman. Their rationale continued: every school has a valedictorian speak. We were special.

These were popular brats elected by the moronic hoards standing between me and my earned spot… and the clown administration was taking them seriously. Louis was a solid C student coasting through classes and passed by teachers subservient to the sports department. He had been handed a full ride at a top tier school. I'm sure his goal was a generic business degree with an express train into the NFL. And he was being handed what I rightfully earned.

I took my appeal to the school board.

"It is absurd to think that something so commonplace as athletic excellence," I said into the microphone on the podium at the very next school board meeting, "something so fleeting that many of the most promising athletes never finish their first year of college due to injury, should cause us to abandon tradition… should dismiss the hard work of those most excelling within our educational system." I had practiced the intoned pleading for days before the meeting.

I filled every second of my speaking minute with a rational appeal to institutional customs and a plea for mercy. The applause from the gathered community only bolstered my cause. No one in administration or school government knew I would speak, so I was met with no organized counterpoint. Most of the adults at the meeting that night was from other towns, so, other than losing to Louis constantly over the last four years, they hadn't known about his coup.

I was called to the principal's office the next day.

He had spent the morning on the phone with various board members and the District's Superintendent. "They told me about your speech last night," he said. "They were led to believe the School Council's request was a done deal."

"I was told that it was," I said.

"But you never talked to me about it."

I said nothing. I had not. The fact that this farce was being taken seriously was proof enough that I would be sidelined.

He continued, "They understood the situation better once I had the opportunity to fully explain the reasonings for the request."

I had been outflanked. Power always protects its own.

"I offered a solution and the board agreed. Louis will speak at graduation in place of the class president. Then the valedictorian will speak."

"Does Beth know?" Beth had been the loudest voice to replace me with Louis. She also happened to be class president. The pieces fell into place. I had somehow stupidly missed the grand scheme. Beth knew people wanted Louis to speak. The popular person's spot was class president. If he spoke, she wouldn't. She was protecting herself and I'd missed it all.

"She does." And that was that. I left his office and began preparing for my five minutes in the spotlight. Beth's glare every time she saw me through the end of the year was the most glorious bonus.

***

"I stand here, today, humbled to be speaking for you," Louis spoke awkwardly into the microphone. His voice echoed throughout the gym. Chairs had been set within the basketball court's boundaries to seat the ninety-eight graduates and their parents in front of the portable stage. The bleachers had been pulled out and filled with extended family members.

"Beth, thank you so much for allowing me to speak today." Louis greeted the administration before continuing the most generic speech I've ever heard about the promises of tomorrow if only we stood and laid the foundation of a new world. That sort of crap. He really leaned into his own hero myth.

He received pre-planned applause and cheers while stretching his five minutes into fifteen. When he finally sat down, he had said very little of real value.

I hadn't cut my hair since ninth grade. My black hair fell between my shoulder blades. The girls in the lunch crew would let me lie in their laps and they would play with it. I often found braids in my hair after lunch. At first, I would pull the braids out. I stopped doing that after the first few months. I thought they were cool, and it made me feel different. Superior. The pleebs would laugh, but their ridicule was beneath me.

For graduation, I had to pull it into a ponytail.

I walked to the podium and cleared my throat. "Doctor Roche, members of the School Board, Principal Walker, Administration, Staff, and my fellow students, we have achieved the first of many milestones in our lives. We have faced turmoil…" I scanned the faces of the graduating class and watched the mood become somber.

"…tragedy…" My eyes met with Alison's. She smiled: her eyes wet.

"…and challenges. And we have stood strong in the face of adversity. We have, each of us, become our own hero. Some of us did so through feats of strength." There was a whoop from the crowd. Then cheers. I paused until they stopped.

"Many of us fought our own, quiet battles. Sometimes we failed. Others, we prospered. Some…" I felt a lump rise in my throat as if on command. "Some fell along the way.

"Still, we move forward.

"As we step away from the safety of our homes, our peers, and our community, we each must choose our own path. For some, that path will take us on to higher education and careers beyond. For others, honorably serving your country in the Armed Forces. Nearly twelve percent of our graduating class, three times the national average, have enrolled.

"More still will move directly into careers and apprenticeships. We must, each of us, plot our course forward as we seize the reins of tomorrow." I paused for effect. I could feel the reverb through the bleachers. My voice dominated the room. It was incredible.

"We must take with us the lessons of yesterday and temper it in the knowledge we gain tomorrow. While our strength will fade, our vision for our world will not. Our intellect will carry us forward. If not for the pursuit of heaven on earth, progress could never be made. Our hope feeds our will. Our will shapes our destiny." I felt larger than life. I had never spoken in public before. Whatever I was to do in life, it had to be filled with this feeling.

"My friends, we are the shapers of tomorrow. No matter where our paths carry us, I ask of you only this.

"Remember the divine intellect and allow it to guide you. We were given a mind and free will setting us above all other things in creation.

"No matter your faith. No matter your political alignment. Trust your unique ability to reason. Forge your own path. Make a new world.

"And congratulations to us all."

Chapter Four

1600. That's the perfect SAT score. That put me in the top twenty-five hundredths of a percent. That and my AP credit hours through my school districts accelerator programs had me beginning as a sophomore on a full academic scholarship to a very prestigious Ivy League school. It was the education that I had earned.

I had been on an early path into advanced chemistry when I felt the rush of leadership that day at graduation. Public service felt the more natural course for me. My university had one of the best schools of political science. I double majored in that and religious studies. I felt that I needed to not only understand how to communicate to the masses, but to understand the most effective and universal method of communication.

But my sights were beyond the foundational study. Diplomacy and law were my ultimate goals.

I was away from home for the first time ever and completely responsible for my daily life. This mostly didn't feel like much of a change. Most of my days were either in class, at work, or home alone. My mom spent most of her days working double shifts to make sure we kept a roof over our heads. While the move had me without a job for the first time since my mid-teens, my life was basically class and dorm room.

If anything, it felt crowded. I had a roommate. Carlos. So, "alone" time was mostly me at a computer or lying in the bed watching television trying to ignore his existence. Social interaction was becoming more and more a challenge.

But the laundry didn't get done on its own. And I had a half mile walk for every meal. It was the first time I'd fully realized how much lifting my mom did for me. I was poised to make all that change. I needed to do for myself while maintaining the grades I needed to keep my scholarships each semester.

I began my first semester with a full schedule of core classes. I finished my basic courses high school, so my first day of college slung me into the academic deep end.

American Politics and Continental Political Thought were my heavy hitters on Tuesdays and Thursdays. I started my Mondays and Wednesdays with Confucian Political Philosophy which counted toward both majors. Religion and Existentialism and Comparative Religions rounded out my week. My advisor, Rence Price, warned me against burning out early, but I needed the credits and would have lost part of my scholarship if I didn't maintain fulltime coursework.

"When I first met you," Carlos started one Thursday afternoon as he returned from a shower. He was getting ready for yet another night out and about. It was the fourth week of the semester and he had managed to party more than half of every week and disappear home every weekend. To be fair, I did very much enjoy his absence. But the three A.M. bursts through the door made morning classes a pain.

"When I first met you, I thought you were going to be a fun guy."

"What do you mean?" I responded.

"Long hair. Thought you were down to party. But you never go out," he said. "You ever have any fun?"

Carlos's usual method of initiating conversation was usually a belch or fart followed by an adolescent chuckle. He was apparently feeling social.

"I… read." It was awkward when I said it. He guffawed.

"You spend your free time reading? Seriously?"

"It helps me relax." I had a copy of Camus' The Stranger on the desk next to my metal-framed bed. I had planned to speed read it that night. We were reading it for class, and I liked being ahead of the discussions.

"You should come out," he said buttoning up one of his flannel shirts and rolling up his sleeves.

"What?" The question caught me off guard. I loathed the thought of being in a crowd, but curiosity got the better of me. "Where do you go?"

"We usually hang out at this house off campus. Most of the jocks find their way there sooner or later." It was football season again. While my school wasn't a national contender, people still loved their excuses to behave irresponsibly.

"Sounds awful," I groaned and reached for my book.

"Nah, man. It's not good for you to always be on. Sometimes, you just gotta unplug." My advisor's words. Seeing my hand hesitate on the book, he continued. "It's walking distance. Give it a chance. If you figure it's not for you, just leave."

I thought about the stories the kids had from the lake each weekend. I remembered how I always overheard them but was never invited to attend. I thought about this new world in which I found myself. I concluded that hiding away would only backfire

"Okay," I said.

***

The house was an older four bedroom on the back side of the bar district. Ghetto adjacent. Six students rented it. Only two of the six knew each other before moving in together. They all worked odd jobs. Three were servers at a posh restaurant downtown. One worked at Kinkos. One was a cook at a diner. And the other tended bar.

The house overflowed with people dropping in, acting ridiculous, and bouncing to other parties or bars. There were all walks of life billowing out of the house. I stood in the corner people watching. A few rich frat boys dropped in, went into one of the rooms, and left about thirty minutes later. There was a band practicing in the garage. I could hear their mediocre music despite the blaring radio and the equally blaring cacophony of conversations.

This older guy wandered in. No one seemed to notice as he made his way into the kitchen and fished three beers from the fridge before walking back out again.

"Want a beer?" Carlos had been sitting on the couch talking to a couple of his friends. He stood and almost yelled the question in my face because the room was so loud.

"Um… I'm not…" I had tasted beer when I was younger. My dad had left one sitting on the table for a few minutes and I slipped a swig. It was awful. "I don't drink beer."

"They have other stuff in there. Come on." He motioned and walked into the kitchen. I followed.

It shouldn't have been possible, but the kitchen was

more crowded than the living room. Carlos pushed a path through to a guy standing by a blender. When he turned the blender off, Carlos leaned in and shouted to the guy. "My friend doesn't like beer. Got anything else?"

The guy grabbed a cup and poured some of the frosty concoction for me. I drank. It was awful. The heat of the alcohol burned a path down my throat to my stomach. I held down the reactionary vomit that threatened its way out. I swallowed hard.

"Good?" Carlos asked.

I smiled and gave him a thumbs up before making my way back out to my corner. Fearing the repercussions of pouring the drink down the drain, I stood holding it. Carlos returned with two beers and rejoined his friends. Each time he looked my way to make sure I was still there I took a sip.

After a while, the heat faded, and the drink didn't taste so foul. Then my lips started to tingle. My tongue dried and swelled filling my mouth making talking impossible. To wet my mouth, I drank more.

Focusing became hard. I didn't even realize my vision was blurred until the door opened and grabbed my attention. It was just some random dude and his girlfriend, but the door opening felt more pronounced somehow. The world seemed to move by slower and slower. I turned my head, and everything went out of focus. My mind looped finding concentration impossible. I mentally grasped for any solid thought hoping to stabilize myself.

I failed.

Blinking seemed to sharpen my sight, so I did that a little more than was natural. It helped.

I staggered my way back into the kitchen. I found the blender still had at least a glass more of the concoction, so I poured myself another.

I found myself leaning into the corner. I wasn't exactly sure how I had gotten there, but my drink was halfway gone, and I didn't see Carlos or his friends anymore. I had really spaced out.

I no longer felt secure. The party seemed to close in on me. I was surrounded by people I didn't know… not that I really knew my roommate either. I began plotting my escape.

Leading with my forehead as if I were diving through a portal a la Donnie Darko, I staggered past strangers to the kitchen. I found the overflowing garbage can and tossed in my empty cup.

No one seemed to notice as I slipped out and headed toward the dorms. The night air was cool, so I breathed in deeply chilling my lungs. That helped to pull me back to reality and hold me here. I probably looked like a lunatic breathing deeply while blinking my eyes far too many times.

A stray cat darted from its hiding place knocking over a trashcan not more than seven feet from me. The adrenaline from that kept me sharp enough to get back to the dorms without issue. It also kept me aware enough to cover the wet portion of the front of my pants.

Had the cat startled me? Had it happened while I was standing in the corner? Even worse, had anyone seen me piss myself?

Back in my dorm, I fell into my bed, and the world spun. Every time I closed my eyes, I felt reality slide from under me. I had to open my eyes and grip the sides of my bed no less than three times. Even though I was lying still, the bed nearly bucked me.

I don't know how long it was that I tried to will myself sober, but I passed out at some point.

Dawn struck with a death gong in my skull.

I couldn't make my classes that Friday. As I lay in bed between sprints to the communal restroom, I reflected on the night before. The powerlessness of it all. My dulled mental faculties became a prison. A regression. A place where I was trapped as a witch emerged from a dimensional gate hidden within a toolbox in an old woman's barn. A place where I cowered beneath covers hoping to fool a man angry at his very existence wanting a scapegoat. Trapped between asphalt and the handlebars of a bike, my legs entangled in bars and chain, watching the dog that drug me down disappear forever.

Never again would I feel that way.

***

That weekend gave me pause. Carlos, as always, went home for the weekend. As I made my way to lunch that Saturday, his words repeated in my mind. Long hair. Thought you were down to party.

I had forgotten my hair. I stopped paying attention to it so many years before that I hadn't paid attention to the new world around me. While I ate a turkey sub and chips in the general cafeteria, I finally looked around at the people. None of the men had long hair. All of them in my political science classes had short hair and were clean shaven. Most wore collared shirts and some even wore neck ties. There were some oddballs in my religious studies classes, but I realized that presentation was paramount.

I finished my sandwich and left campus. I wandered until I found a barber shop. This being a college town on the weekend, they weren't busy. I was sat almost immediately.

"What're we doing today?" the barber asked as he brushed some tangles out of my long locks.

The walls around the mirrors were peppered with all sorts of headshots showing different styles. I found a short, professional-looking cut and pointed at it. "That."

He looked at the photo and at me. "Yeah. I can see that." He inspected my head of hair for a bit, pointed to a curl toward the front, and spoke again, "We go too short, and that part will most likely stand up. But I think I can make it work. You sure? Big change."

"Definitely."

By the time he was finished, his floor was coated with shimmering black hair and the back of my neck prickled under the first breeze it had felt in years. I rubbed the short hairs on the back of my head. It felt weird, but it felt good. I smiled and paid the guy.

From the barber, I walked to the bank and checked my account. I had been stashing every bit of money I could, and I still had some remaining funds from my scholarships tucked away. It wasn't a lot, but I could make do.

I made my way to a men's consignment shop where I spent about three hundred dollars on new outfits. Three pairs of dress slacks, seven collared shirts of various pastels, and, under the advice of one of the clerks there, two belts and two pairs of shoes – one black and one brown.

Back in my dorm, I washed, dried, and hung my new clothes before bundling my older tee shirts and jeans and moving them to the bottom drawers. Those would only come out when I was slumming around the dorm room or going home for a visit.

When Monday rolled around, I was a new man ready for a new world.

In addition to being my advisor, Rence was a grad student and the teacher's assistant for Continental Politics. I could see the surprise on his face when he noticed me. He usually seemed almost burdened every time I came to class. It almost felt like he was hoping I'd burn out and leave school.

But his demeanor changed. The lack of recognition on his face when he first saw the stranger with neatly styled hair, striped button-down shirt, and bottle green herringbone tweed pants spoke volumes. The shocked realization when it finally hit him was the cherry on top. I realized how very true the maxim: clothes make the man.

I dove deep into my studies. The competition for the top seat was infinitely more intimidating than high school had ever been. Back then, I soared effortlessly above my peers. I was a florescent rose in a field of dandelions. Here… here I was one of many seals in a sea of many, many sharks… and I desperately wanted to become a shark.

"Quinn!" Rence called after class one day. We were in the finals stretch… that time closer to finals than to midterms… and I was blowing it out of the park. Doctor Haddish had already pulled me aside. I had proposed, as my year-end thesis topic, the strategic increase in the coupling of strategy between business interests and the religious right. He was fascinated by the concept and wanted me to explore the theoretical execution of such a strategy. He suggested that if the paper delivered as well as the pitch, I could explore publication. After that, Rence's focus was exclusively on any coattails I may offer. "What are you doing this weekend?"

"The usual," I answered. Between this paper and preparing for all my other finals, I spent nearly every free minute between the campus's library and the large Catholic church's collection. Haddish had pulled some strings and got me access even though I was neither clergy nor Catholic.

"Pause that for Saturday. I have an opening for a waiter at this fund raiser at Haddish's golf club."

"Why on earth would I want to do that?" I couldn't fathom Rence would belittle me so much as to imply I had to demean myself for Haddish's approval.

"Trust me, man. Governor Hall is making a silent announcement for his re-election kick off. Haddish just might show you off. Worst case you network a little."

The idea of having a strategy session with the sitting governor flashed through my mind. "Hall is going to be there?"

"Yeah. It's an unofficial official announcement before he formally confirms his re-election campaign. Haddish put me on coordinating the catering staff, so I get to be there. But one of the waiters quit and she can't replace them with people who could go through a background check in time. So, I told her I had someone."

Opportunity. Always seize it.

I agreed.

***

Saturday night rolled around. I entered through the staff entry like Rence had told me to and checked in with Cathy, the rather large and very mean wait staff wrangler.

"Have you ever waited tables?" She barked.

"I've carried dishes, yes."

She cursed at me and ran through the basics of the menu and how I was expected to take orders. I did as I was told as I worked my assigned tables. They stuck me in the corner nearest the kitchen and never on an intercept path with the Governor's table where Haddish and Rence sat. That table was exclusively going to this girl who was significantly more attractive than she was skilled.

The clubhouse was furnished with twenty ten-person round tables. It was elegantly decorated with crystal place settings and expensive linens. It wasn't quite black tie but might as well have been. I recognized several state lawmakers and a couple national folks. I'd later learn there were wealthy businessmen and organizational leaders from around the region in attendance.

The wealthiest person at my tables was a Russian soybean farmer. He owned thousands of acres and was some bigwig in domestic biodiesel production. He sat around popping back vodka shots all night and laughing loudly at his own jokes. The gorgeous woman half his age sitting next to him was his wife. When he wasn't looking, she wore repulsion on her face. I guess the money was just too good.

The night got to be a bit too much for Cathy, so she and a couple others, including Hall's waitress, slipped out the back for a break. She hadn't returned when the soup course for the main table hit the line. I took it out.

I slid Haddish's bowl in front of him. He followed the strange hand up and locked onto my face. He lit up with what looked almost like pride.

"Jeffery!" he called. "Hey, Jeffery!" I followed his eyes three seats down to where Governor Jeffery Hall was sitting. "I want you to meet someone." He stood and took the platter of bowls from my hands. He nodded to Rence who called the first waiter they saw. After handing the soups off, he hooked his fingers around my arm just above my elbow and guided me.

"This is Quinn Constance. The one I was telling you about."

"Okay, yeah," Hall remembered. He turned to me. "Haddish told me about some of your strategic ideas. I'd love to… Are you waiting tables?"

"I am.

"Well, stop that for now. Have a seat with us." Hall nodded to the man sitting next to him and they moved their chairs around the table allowing me to pull one up next to the Governor. It turned out the older man sitting next to Hall was Jordan Twine, Hall's chief campaign strategist.

"So, tell me about this strategy of yours."

Haddish patted me on the shoulder and returned to his seat. I knew he would be listening intently, but he was signaling that I was on my own.

I stammered to start a few times. Hall held up a hand for me to stop. "I'm not grading you here. We're having a conversation. Talk to me like you would anyone else."

I breathed deeply and exhaled. "Sorry." I composed myself before telling the Governor about my religious history. I bounced from church to church, Catholic to Baptist to Methodist, until I found my way to a non-denominational church family near the end of high school.

My connection to the various churches pretty much dried up immediately after high school and served as little inspiration for my daily life at that time. There were some messages of hope, but most of it was filled with overwhelming guilt for being alive and I found that part of the faith utterly useless.

But there was something inspirational in the message of the non-denominational church. This growing evangelism shrugged off the authority of denominational diversity and carved a new path forward with a divine entitlement to leadership. The movement was growing.

Hall recognized exactly what I was saying. "That is a huge voting block in this state," he said after I'd rambled for a while.

I became a bit over animated. His acknowledgment made me feel like my ideas were on a more stable foundation than I had assumed. "That's what I'm talking about! The movement is growing exponentially. And I believe that political thought can grow in a similar manner. If a political idea can spark the same entitlement… the same sense of divine

correctness… it will be a force to be reconned with."

The Governor thought about this for a few minutes.

"That is disturbing," was his immediate response. My guts fell into my knees. "The last thing we would want to do is invite these power-hungry preachers in and grant them influence. Proper governance demands compromise. These zealots give nothing."

"I'm not saying to give them influence, per say," I attempted to correct. "It is their methodology that I find fascinating. And there are so many versions of organized religions, pretty much anywhere on the political spectrum can saddle up a denomination and ride.

"Take my old church for example. They organize financial planning groups and solicit tithing promising financial growth. They outreach through a motorcycle club, and they have another club for reviewing movies. None of these openly tell people they're religious in nature and they are expanding. Then the leaders slip in Biblical talking points."

"I don't…" he began, but I interrupted.

"The point is messaging couched within other things people are interested in. The church itself saw a thirty-six percent increase in revenue the last two years I was there. And the social circles have expanded beyond the old prayer chains. The church is connected to the surrounding three town councils and has placed after-school programs in five schools in two districts." I pause for effect. "They've mastered the art of magnifying influence. I believe these strategies can be applied to influencing public opinion at just about every level of government. This would amplify Nixon's southern strategy…"

He held up his hand stopping me. That's when I noticed his smile.

"It was good meeting you, Quinn. Enjoy the rest of the party," he said before standing. He nodded to Jordan before leaving the table to greet other diners.

I was dumbfounded. I wanted to follow. I wanted to ask him what he thought. But, when I stood to pursue, Jordan placed a meaty hand on my shoulder.

"Are you interested in a little internship over the summer?" he asked.

"I… uh… I'm still just a freshman."

"Should that really matter?"

Opportunity again. Never shy away.

"Where?"

Jordan told me about a large house outside of DC where future influencers and thought leaders networked and served the powerful. Lawmakers. Businessmen. Foreign nationals. He said it would be good for me. Three months then back to school. He told me to keep working on the paper and handed me his card instructing me to email it to him once it's ready.

He clapped me hard on the back and walked away joining a group of people congregating outside the dining room. A football game played on the television mounted behind the bar out there. I watched the crowd cheering in unison. It was late in the semester. Must have been a championship game or something.

I reluctantly followed. Standing at the back of the crowd, I looked on curiously.

"Football fan?" The woman's voice was sweet yet deep.

"I don't really follow it," I replied. I turned and saw a beautiful brunette with deep green eyes. Even though she couldn't have been any older than me, her conservative dress seemed to add five years to her.

"You've never heard of The Rocket?" She said it almost sarcastically.

"The who?"

She chuckled and walked past me toward the bar. I followed.

She pushed her way through the crowd and ordered a hard cider. "Wait, are you old enough to…"

She looked at me and smiled offering her hand to shake. "Celeste Hall."

"Hall?"

"Yeah," she smiled. "You were talking with my father earlier."

I had no time to respond before she continued. "You mean to tell me you don't know the biggest name in college football? Some sort of freshman super man. They say he plays baseball, too."

"Wait." Reality seemed to contort around me. I scrambled past a few people clustered around the bar and looked intently at the screen finding what I desperately hoped I would not. The graphic beneath the replay footage of a Hail Mary pass read: Louis "The Rocket" Bryant.

Louis had found his way to Auburn and managed national recognition long before the end of the football season. Somewhere along the way, everyone began calling him The Rocket. He could launch the ball faster and farther than any other player and, when he decided to run, he would blast through every defensive line. He was the youngest Heisman candidate ever.

"You look disgusted," Celeste said in my ear. "You're really not a football fan."

"Not really a Louis Bryant fan, if I'm honest."

"You know him?"

"Same hometown," I answered.

"I know a few guys around here who'd love to shake your hand for that reason alone."

"Gross," I said. I looked around. The last thing I wanted was to be submerged in a sea of fools cheering for Louis. "I need to go. It was nice meeting you, Celeste." I shook her hand and made my way to the exit.

***

"And where did you disappear to?" Rence quizzed when he found me deep in the library later that weekend. I looked up from one of many thick books to see his smug, smiling face. He sat across the table from me and continued. "You were quite the shining star."

"Hardly," I answered and looked back to my book hoping he would take the hint that I didn't want to be bothered with company.

"Why'd you leave? Haddish was looking for you. He said you made quite an impression. That internship you landed… well… we can't all be hand selected I guess." The venom in his voice betrayed his jealousy. At the time, I had no clue exactly what the internship was. It sounded like a janitorial job. Servicing the powerful didn't sound like my idea of career development.

I slid my marker into the book, closed it, and placed it on the table. "What's the deal with this internship? I was planning to go home for the summer and, frankly, haven't decided to accept."

Rence chuckled arrogantly. "This is what happens when you just disappear." He stood to leave. "See Haddish during office hours on Monday," he added.

I spent the rest of the weekend pushing forward on my paper. The encounter with the Governor and the secrecy of this internship had me keen to polish it as soon as I could.

That Monday, I visited Haddish.

"Not a football fan?" he asked after I entered.

"I'm sorry?"

"Celeste mentioned you left during the game."

"It tends to be a bit tribalistic for me… chanting and cheering for brutes whose sole purpose in life is to ram into each other."

"For someone so keen to apply might-makes-right to political battles, you far too easily discount physical prowess."

"Political leadership uses the physical battle as a tool, nothing more."

"Untrue. The physical battle is a tool that helps align public sentiment with political leadership."

I thought about that. I remembered the Desert Storm cheerleading from the major news networks and how there seemed to almost be unanimous public support for the administration at that time. Haddish wasn't wrong.

"Sit down," he said. I did. "How's the paper coming?"

"Good," I reassured him. "I should be ready to submit by the end of the week."

"No need. I've recorded the six." I was stunned. Six was out of six possible points. This meant I'd secure my four-oh. That meant I'd see a thirty percent increase in next year's scholarship funding, and I would be in competition for two sizeable academic grants.

"I thought…"

"You fully exhibited knowledge of the subject matter with the Governor. He was impressed," Haddish interrupted.

"He argued with me."

"Hall is a more traditional politician. A Reananite. Christians were a large part of the Civil Rights push. Mostly black churches. But Nixon couldn't villainize them like he could the Black Panthers and the hippies." I knew the history. Nixon silenced the churches by threatening to tax them if they were politically active. Through his southern strategy, he empowered white, right-wing Christianity and used state force to wipe out anti-capitalists and anti-racists like X and King. But the Reaganites felt church leadership wasn't fully aligned with business interests. Hall was with the camp still nervous about reaching out to the fundamentalists.

I knew better.

"He doesn't agree with you, but he was intrigued. And you demonstrated a solid grasp on your position. Being recommended for Ivanwald is huge. Their membership represents the best of the best."

Ivanwald. I had read about its association with C-Street and very powerful people around the world. They guided the most powerful men and women in business and government. Influencers. Power brokers. A hidden powerhouse of string pullers and leaders of religious thought.

And I would be spending my summer with them.

***

Ivanwald changed my life. From the hours of four in the morning to eleven at night, the mansion surged with activity. Short prayers before pre-dawn work outs. Group breakfasts and dinners. Drinks. Socializing.

And through the middle of the day, we networked with each other and with those we served. The group consisted of writers and actors, influencers and the adult children of early tech millionaires or mega-pastors. We came from more than twenty nations. We were the emerging shapers of tomorrow.

We spent our nights reading, conversing, and sleeping two to a room in the large, Arlington-area mansion that was Ivanwald. I met men from completely different backgrounds with completely different outlooks on life. But we all seemed to meet with a single intent.

Our days were spent living humbly in service to true power. We understood the divine nature earthly power. We knew that man was handed dominion over the land and animals, and we knew any society created by mankind was guided into creation by the hand of God. Leadership was ordained. We were the chosen future of humanity.

Until then, we cleaned gutters and toilets and prepared and served food for socials attended by the most powerful business leaders and politicians around the world. The Speaker of the House, third in line for the U.S. Presidency, knew me by name before the end of the first month.

Governor Hall was well known in corridors of Ivanwald and throughout C-Street, a lobbying office in DC run by the Family; the group behind all of this. The group not only included the puppets, but the pullers of the puppets' strings. Both major US political parties were well represented.

There were rumblings of other-worldly powers developing in Africa circulating by the end of the summer. Two of the Ivanwald attendees, Bale and Mukasa, were twin sons of the Ugandan dictator, Dende Akello. The twins received a letter from their mother. The Akello family ran one of the largest megachurches in Africa out of the Presidential compound. The sanctuary was literally next to the war room. It was the perfect unification of Church and State.

The letter told of a man who had been run over by a bus who then stood, without injury, after it was moved off him. She told a story of him being shot but healing immediately after. She called it a miracle.

The twins laughed at the letter. "Our mother is so gullible," Bale said. "She once paid this psychic to commune with her dead father and advise her in how best to invest the fortune he left her. The psychic convinced my mother to pour it all into a church in his hometown. It just so happened the psychic's family ran the church."

"Father had him shot in front of the palace and then sent the military to seize the church and reclaim the stolen wealth," Mukasa added.

Bale tossed the letter onto the table with a laugh. I grabbed it up and read. I saw something a little different hidden in the letter's subtext. I saw public spectacle. I saw a growing challenge to Akello's authority. And I told them so.

"Do you really believe there is a threat?" Mukasa asked.

"Maybe not right now, but if this charlatan can fool your mother, I'm sure he can fool others. He must be plotting something. People don't go through this sort of effort for nothing. I would warn your father to be mindful of him."

The twins looked at me skeptically but followed my recommendation. Dende Akello jailed the charlatan for blasphemy. To my knowledge, he never released the man.

<u>Chapter Five</u>

I earned my two bachelor's degrees within the next two and a half years. I graduated summa cum laude with a nearly perfect GPA. With recommendation letters from the offices of several state and national lawmakers, I had my choice of law schools.

Along the way, Celeste and I began dating. I returned to my mother's house from Ivanwald two days before classes began my second semester. I had very little time to find a place to live, buy my books, and move back to campus. Interestingly, it had all been taken care of, and all I needed to do was kiss my mother goodbye and drive into the city. I moved into an upscale building near campus a Senator owned. He had mentioned he could take care of housing if I needed. I just hadn't thought he was serious. It was on the bottom floor and near the elevators. Probably why it was vacant. But he had set my rent far below the regular rate and let me slide on deposit and first and last month's rent… a usual requirement to even view a unit in this building. I was reaping the benefits of service.

The key was waiting for me in a lockbox in the main office. When I got to the apartment, I found my belongings and the books and supplies for all of my classes already there. I would unpack slowly over the next week. But, living in the center of the heart of the seat of power in this state had its perks. The delivery options were far superior to everything around campus. The neighbors were older, so it was quiet… quieter than I'd ever heard.

People laugh when I say that. "But you grew up on a farm," they all would inevitably quip. "How is anything quieter than a farm." Don't let Hollywood fool you. Farms are loud. When the domesticated animals go to roost, a cacophony of screaming madness begins. Cicadas. Owls. Rodents. Things moving about in the woods beyond the clearing. Things that hunt at night. I sat by my open window as a child unable to sleep thanks to the noise.

This place was silent. It was well built, so I never heard my neighbors. No conversations. No walking around upstairs. I lived in that apartment through undergrad and the three additional years of law school. I lived there as I earned one academic achievement after another. I lived there when I clerked for the Chief Justice of the Supreme Court in law school. I lived there when Celeste and I met for the second time at her father's inauguration after winning his second term as Governor. I lived there when I interned my last semester with Hagee & Bess, the largest PR firm catering to almost every nationally recognized politician, A-list actor, and several top athletes. And I lived there when Hagee & Bess, while pursuing the top NFL draft, learned that I had a personal history with The Rocket himself, Louis Bryant.

Louis had coasted through his college career landing a liberal arts degree in philosophy or psychiatry or some hippie-dippie crap. I doubt he was overly challenged seeing as he has been the only player in history to win three Heisman trophies and the College World Series Most Outstanding Player award twice. When I said top draft pick, I meant of all time. There I was at a minimally paid internship earning credits toward my bachelor's degree, and Louis whirlwinds back into my life.

The firm desperately wanted to represent The Rocket. He was expected to be the first billion-dollar athlete in NFL history. The marketing wrote itself. They wanted something unique, and they wanted to lock Louis down. Martin Trent, the Operations VP who wrangled the interns, matched The Rocket's hometown with mine from background checks. The graduation dates matching was enough to get me on the chief partners' radar. I was assigned to the team charged with closing the deal.

It was truly divine intervention. More than that, it was an opportunity. As little as I cared to reunite with my high school rival, I suddenly saw a way to hitch my earned fortune to his rising stardom.

We were the last of five agencies The Rocket was interviewing. We were the top contender. Our brand was unmatched.

We met Louis and his mother, her name was Kent by then, at the Pratt Steakhouse. It was the posh of the posh. Formalwear only. No one ate there for less than three hundred dollars a head. There were five of us on our side of the table. The Rocket, his mother, and his stepfather on his.

The surprise on Louis's face when introductions were made, and he saw me was exhilarating. The wind of the room blew across my face with the speed he used pulling me from a handshake into a crushing hug. For a fraction of a second, I felt like I was riding a bike again.

I had to tap out before I passed out. He had grown into a behemoth of a man.

"Mom! You remember Quinn, don't you?" The happiness in his voice was almost childlike. Had he suffered too many concussions already? Was I setting up a hundred-million-dollar public relations contract with a dead man?

Mrs. Bryant… er… Kent… wore a smile betraying a scowl. I could see reflections of a Graduation Day insult in her eyes. "I do," she monotoned.

We sat and ate and told stories from our childhood to the table. Nostalgia works better than psilocybin for shaving away the haze of faded memories. The years fall away.

Well into the third hour of the evening, with the main course and dessert behind us, it was finally time for business. The table was swimming in drinks. I stuck to soda water.

Jacob, the lead on the team, took point and directly made his pitch. Sponsorships. Commercial gigs. Name and likeness licensing. Easily a billion dollars in five years. The Rocket deserved the best, and Hagee & Bess was the best.

Louis's stepfather leaned in. His voice betrayed that, just like Jacob, he had been nursing his drinks allowing them to water themselves down before finishing only one. "You're not offering us anything new. Louis's talent will close all those deals with little effort from a PR firm. What makes your offer different from anyone else?"

The sales team lost the plot. They stumbled realizing for the very first time this dinner wasn't a done deal. They had never planned for this contingency. Amateurs pulling down eight figures a year.

I had.

"An image," I chimed in. The table turned toward me.

"He has an image," the stepfather countered.

"Sure. All American. Small town born. Humble roots. No public misconduct. He has a perfectly flawless image. A little too flawless. People can't see themselves in Louis. He's going to be brightly burning meteor disintegrating long before it should. He will have years of playing on a boring image having to re-invent himself every few years to stay relevant. No one likes perfect."

By this time, my superiors were glaring holes in my forehead trying to get me to shut up. I ignored them and pressed forward.

"I'm not saying Louis doesn't match that image. Of course, he does. I can attest to that." And again, I lied. This pretense was sickening. But I was in survival mode and would not fail because these novices couldn't even bring their C-game. "But the people need to be able to identify. The western hero's journey is subconsciously enshrined within the mind of every red-blooded American. And Louis has a real-life story of heroism."

The mood changed. My co-workers leaned forward, intrigued. So did the stepfather. Even his mother's mood shifted. Big reveal. I told the story of Louis and the fiery crash. The night Louis Bryant became a hero. Everyone who sees him would see their own heroic potential. He will be the new American Myth.

"That woman you saved on the bridge still lives in that same house, right? Her daughter would be five by now? We can make your signing a reunion event. You can be the real-life Captain America."

"I've told him his entire life that he was a real hero. Every time he struggled in school. Every missed pass and imperfect play. Getting through the loss of his father…" Mrs. Kent choked on those words swallowing before continuing. "He faced adversity every day. But, in it all, he is a hero."

I cringed with the words faced adversity. Louis Bryant had no clue what adversity truly meant.

My team was silent. While I focused on the parents and how excited they were for the plan, they watched Louis's souring face.

"I avoid talking about that, Quinn. I'd have thought

you, of all people, would know that."

How could I have known that? Had he said it in any number of interviews I never watched? Had he ever confided in me that he pretended to hate what made him better than everyone else? I hadn't been in his life in any real sense since seventh grade. How was I supposed to know what silly hang ups he had?

Louis and his parents argued. They wanted him to think about it. He refused. My superiors glared at me. I watched them through my peripheral vision as I stared at the table. This career path had just ended.

"Thank you, gentlemen, for the dinner." Louis ended the argument by standing. He offered his hand. The team lead shook it and apologized. "It's fine. I just don't think we're the right fit for your firm. Thank you, again."

He left. His parents followed.

We stood around the table in silence. "If you have any property in the Hagee & Bess office, get it out before Monday," the team lead growled into my ear as they filed out.

***

The gubernatorial election was the semester I returned from Ivanwald and Hall won re-election handily. His conservative, pro-business administration was exactly what a right-to-work state needed. And the people knew it.

Everyone in the governor's camp knew where to find me, so I wasn't surprised when the invitation to the inaugural ball arrived. I wondered if I would have a chance to talk to Hall about my ideas and how I was even more convinced I was right after my summer with the Family.

I never got that chance. When Hall arrived, it was late, and he was whisked in. He shared a dance with his wife and was back out the door within an hour. But Celeste was there the entire night. She was responsible for planning the event. That was her talent. Every detail was a part of the spectacle of every event she staged. A true artiste.

She found me not long after I'd arrived. "Oh my god, what are you wearing?" she asked as a greeting. She giggled.

"I… uh…" I stammered looking myself up and down. I was in a standard black suit and white shirt. My shoes, I knew, were polished. The only color I wore was in my tie and socks.

"I love that pattern!" I had gone into a high-end shop one weekend when I drove up to New York. I found this matching tie and sock set with bright paisley of reds, blues, and greens. She gushed over the odd matching.

I beamed.

We talked about the campaign and the summer and how she was about to return to New York to Parsons School of Design. She introduced me to Representative Jones from my district and I introduced her to Senator Cartilage from Texas. Then she introduced me to Governor Hall's business partner, Jason Malikal.

Their holdings in a network of chemical processing and nuclear waste disposal companies made them two of the wealthiest men in the state. While Hall was governor, Malikal was responsible for the stability and operations of their businesses. The buzz that night was that Malikal would be buying Hall out in six years. Hall was a favorite for the Presidency. His double-digit win margin all but sealed the deal with some of his detractors.

My conversation with Malikal was one of the first times I spoke openly about my desire for law school. Malikal was aware of my time at Ivanwald and quipped that it doesn't sound like it would be "much of a challenge" for me. I couldn't disagree with him. He added that perhaps, if I chose to go into corporate law, I should look him up once I passed the bar.

The entire night was like that. I was stunned by the keen interest in my future many of the powerful people at that ball took.

Celeste had a bit too much to drink. I caught her stumbling to a seat late in the evening.

"Come on," I said and helped her to her feet. "Let me take you home."

She protested, but I convinced her the party would be fine without her. She needed to save face. It was her father's night after all.

I took her to her apartment and ensured she got through her door. When I turned to leave, she reached out and grabbed my arm. "You should ask me out," she said.

The thought hadn't occurred to me. Thinking back on it, I was an idiot. But I was so taken with the night and the celebration and the potential. I smiled. "I will," I said and pulled away. "After you've had a night to sleep." I walked away hearing the door close and lock behind me.

The next day, I checked up on her. As expected, she was miserable. Hungover. But she was sober. And she was packing for Parsons.

"When do you leave?" I asked.

"Next week. Classes begin Thursday."

I told her I hoped she could rid herself of the hangover soon. Then I turned to leave again.

"Weren't you supposed to ask me out?" she asked.

"I wasn't sure you'd remember," I answered. I paused then, "Would you like to go out sometime?"

She laughed. Then winced.

"I'll let you get some rest. Dinner tomorrow night?"

"Absolutely," she answered.

Dinner was amazing. One of the best steaks I ever had. We spent most of our free time over the next few days together. I drove her to New York that Monday and moved her into her apartment.

We spoke to each other every night. When 9/11 happened, she left school and moved home. Eleven months later, she moved in with me.

During the week, we were the typical student couple. She went to a design school nearby and I sailed to two degrees and into law school.

On the weekends, we were the hot, young socialite couple networking with the most powerful businessmen and politicians around the country. We even worked on an envoy group to Russia where we discussed soybean imports and biodiesel production. The deal would bring fifteen hundred new jobs to the state and vastly expand Hall's chemical production and disposal companies. It would give Hall the needed victory to secure his name in the public's mind as he built a Presidential campaign.

The liberal took the White House and Hall was nearing the end of his second term when the world changed.

***

The Rocket took the NFL by storm. He signed with the Patriots in a historic half-billion-dollar, five-year deal. Combined with loads of sponsorships and the marketing of his likeness, Louis would be a billionaire by the end of the season. His PR firm modeled his comic book super-hero image after his near-perfect winning track record.

He was quickly reaching living legend status. His primary home when he wasn't in Boston was a three-bedroom, single-family house near his mother's home. Living modestly, he funneled hundreds of millions of dollars directly into education and healthcare programs in the poorest neighborhoods throughout the state. A true Andy Griffith heart.

At least that's how he was portrayed in the media.

The Rocket had ivory tower status. He and his wife were a new American royalty. Speaking ill of him at that time ended sportscasters' careers. His hands were somehow always clean, though. Public opinion was on his side. He did no wrong. He was the god-head of the cult of The Rocket.

His last game of the season was against the Broncos. According to those who followed the sports, the Broncos were a great team that year. It was set to be an epic game.

In the third quarter, Louis called a play. It was set to be a fake where he tossed the ball laterally and then ran out to catch the pass. Only, the pass went way high and wide. There was no way the catch was happening. And there were defenders bearing down on him hard. It looked like they were going to try to cripple him.

Stories flooded social media by this time. Miracle people did the impossible. Women lifted trucks. Little boys started fires just by looking at them. There was a rumor of a shape changer terrifying southern Yemen. No one knew if it would be a man or a woman or some animal. People feared their own shadows. It ignited a resurgence of horror television and became a digital mythology.

Ever since the Akello boys told me about the Ugandan immortal, these stories became more and more common. However, most of the videos posted online were low quality and hard to make out. Others were clearly faked.

With defenders closing in, The Rocket leaped for the ball. Josh Bartlett was the first to crash into him. His lifeless body collapsed to the field after his neck snapped against The Rocket's immovable shin. The Rocket, live on prime-time Monday Night Football, ball in hand, was flying.

<u>Chapter Six</u>

Over the next few weeks, the world spun out of control. The Rocket seemed as surprised as everyone else. He went into seclusion that first week. He hermitted himself away at home. Private security kept people off the property. His spokespeople were everywhere. There was speculation about how much of his talent had been powers this whole time, accusations that he knew and hid it to enrich himself and talk of manslaughter charges.

Governor Hall joined lawmakers and religious leaders in support of The Rocket. They asked for public calm as information was released, but they believed this represented a turning point for the human species. Potentially, an evolutionary leap forward for us all.

The loons called him the second coming. Apocalyptic preppers had a field day. Overnight, the survivalist industry exploded. Weapons manufacturers re-organized their production to accommodate an exploding small arms market. Several military cease fires were announced around the world.

That second week, Louis emerged from his safe hidey-hole. He was coached but uneasy. His people had convinced him to make a statement. They held a press conference on his front lawn. Behind him, beyond the wall of shrubbery lining his property, I saw my childhood home. After the foreclosure, it had been sold and seemed to be thriving.

"Good afternoon," he started. He sat a typed statement on the podium in front of him. He started without looking down. "To Josh Bartlett's family, I…" he quaked with an unscripted sob. "I am so sorry," he continued after a calming pause. "I didn't know Josh. Over the last week, I was blessed to speak with his family and friends. We spoke about his children, Jenny and Mark. And about his wife, Daphne. From every account…" he paused again. "From every account, Josh was a good man. And he was a great player." He looked down at the podium and picked up a few words from the paper there.

"I am honored to have shared the field with him. What happened last Monday night shocked the world… and it shocked me.

"Never before have I experienced anything like what I did on that field. I always felt I was special… that there was something pushing me forward. I believed my talents were God-given.

"I am not convinced that they aren't." He looked over the crowd. "They are just… so much more… than I ever knew."

"There has been a lot of speculation about these powers… about what they are and what I will do next. The truth is, I don't know where they're from or how I was able to do what I did.

"For now, I have a team of doctors lining up a barrage of tests. I am hoping to better understand what is happening to me.

"I am retiring from the NFL as of immediately. I was taught the value of good sportsmanship at a young age. With my advantages, it wouldn't be right for me to continue playing. The sport of football has been a huge part of my life and I will miss the game, but my life just got a lot more complicated." He chuckled and the press chuckled along with him. They had been prepped. His people didn't miss a beat. After this stunt, his endorsement deals alone would run into the tens of billions of dollars.

"Special abilities do not make me a superior person. No matter what I do next, I am still just a man. I will live as a man should live, in service to his fellow man, to his community, and to his God."

Louis tucked away his note cards. He looked to his people who nodded approvingly. Then he went back inside without answering questions.

***

Hall's last year as governor was tumultuous. Just like every other governor in the country, Hall spoke out in support of The Rocket and his newfound powers. The hero-worship was disgusting.

The gubernatorial primaries were in full swing with Hall's Lieutenant Governor running against a much more conservative State Representative. Hall was sitting out of the primaries saving his endorsement for the winner. With his focus on the presidential exploratory committee, he couldn't risk going too far or too little to the right in his own state.

His presidential prospects were strong. The state's economy was trending stronger than the national one. The current President was more focused on foreign wars than the economy and Hall had a strong showing in the polls against him. It didn't hurt that Hall was known as the nation's strongest against crime... a mantle everyone desired no matter on which side of the aisle they sat.

I was on the back half of law school and was very nearly a part of the family. The expectation was that Celeste and I would get married once I passed the bar. As such, I was added to Hall's Presidential exploratory committee.

One of our first meetings was about three months after the Rocket Revelation, as the media was calling it. The team already had so many polls and statistics to review. It sounded like a numbers game or a Wall Street trading floor, not like a development of ideas.

The evening wasn't sitting well with me.

"Is now not the time to talk strategy?" I blurted after half-an-hour of the nonsense. The room was quiet.

"What did you have on your mind, Quinn?" my future father-in-law broke the silence.

"I don't know. I expected this to be the place where ideas were discussed. Where we mapped the course of the future campaign."

Hall chuckled. "We'll get there. First, we look at the field and where the demographics are, then we'll bring in people to shape the message."

I knew this. I did. This was 101 level stuff. But I always hoped the inner circle of a campaign was more than spreadsheets dramatized by Hollywood.

When he saw my look of disappointment, he continued, "I have a public record, Quinn. Right now, we're seeing how far we expect that record to carry me and where I need to focus different messaging to lock in national prospects."

"But…" I stopped. They didn't care to hear my concerns. I could read it on the others' faces. I was the interloper. The nepotism hire. There were industry leaders and campaign experts from around the country sitting in the room plotting the most bureaucratic political exchange of power I'd been loath to witness. I was still in law school.

"What are you thinking? I wanted you here for a reason," he said.

"I think you're wrong on The Rocket and I think it will sink you."

"What are you talking about?" Jordan Twine incredulously spoke out. "The Rocket is a godsend. Only an idiot would stand against a real American hero."

"Hero?" I asked. I couldn't believe what I was hearing. They truly didn't see it. "Did the media brainwashing make you forget about Josh Bartlett?" The room immediately tensed.

"You're talking about someone guilty of manslaughter, at best, on national television. You're witness to the failure of the justice system as celebrity and idolatry erase the rule of law."

"That's a very fringe way of looking at what happened," Hall interrupted. "Right or not, he is the new bald eagle, a symbol of the American spirit. A hero to the world. Speaking out against him…"

"The Rocket represents the destruction of American greatness." There was a new tension as I interrupted Hall. I was on very thin ice, but I couldn't silence myself.

"Think about it. He's the ultimate Welfare State. A boy scout thriving on a victim society. People will stop doing for each other and for themselves. Instead, they'll rely on the great super-man to save the day."

"Has he shown any desire to be that sort of thing?" someone else in the room blurted. "He's testing his powers and living a life at home with his family."

"It's who Louis is!" I shouted.

Hall stood. "Thank you, Quinn. I know you two have a history. And I don't know if this is something personal. I like to think it's not."

"It…"

He held up a hand and cut me off. "There's no reason to fight this right now. Thank you for your opinion, but we need to get back to work."

I was silenced. We returned to discussing percentage points and recent redistricting that broke up former union strongholds that would skew a certain swing state to the right.

***

Hall was in his last few months as governor. His lieutenant governor was hot on the campaign trail after his primary win and Hall's formal endorsement. Most of this part of his Administration was prepping staff for the change over and packing things to move out of the governor's mansion.

To his credit, Hall allowed me to write opinion pieces against the concept of heroes and the cult of personality, but he would not let me go after The Rocket directly. I did. Not too many of my articles got any traction. Some conspiracy sites latched on to the story and concocted some PSYOP or false flag attack that would bring about a Communist dictatorship –

nonsensical garbage. I was beginning to lose hope in my message.

But then things, once again, changed.

Hall's chemical processing contracts were in the billions of dollars. His overhead costs were low. He and Malikal bought an abandoned industrial park near the harbor for pocket change. They bypassed the need to completely renovate the buildings thanks to previous regulation-busting administrations. Things were very profitable for their first decade in business.

But Hall was to bear witness to the destruction heroes leave in their wake.

A fire broke out in one of their chlorine gas processing facilities. It shouldn't have been a big fire. Easily manageable. But old emergency procedures were still active, and the building went into lockdown. A clog in the waterline feeding the sprinkler system caused catastrophic failure. If it could go wrong, it did.

There were one hundred and thirty-seven people in the building and six-inch steel doors holding them inside to either die by fire or by chlorine gas. And no one could get the doors open.

The national media latched onto the ordeal. Since the factory was just outside DC, the news of the fire went national within a half hour. I was with the Governor watching everything unfold from his office. Someone from one of the crews managed to tap into the CCTV feed, so everyone could witness the terror on the faces of the workers uselessly fighting the growing fire with the ten extinguishers throughout the building. It grew too big and was now threatening the stability of the gas containment system. If the seals melted, the people inside would experience a very painful death.

The Rocket arrived.

He just… appeared. He flew across three states and instantly hovered in the air above the factory. The sonic boom he caused shocked the people on the ground and the television cameras swung wildly searching for the cause. They focused on The Rocket.

He wore a uniform that played tribute to his high school football jersey: a red shirt with a black rocket logo where a number would have typically been. His red tights had thigh and knee pads built in, and he wore red cleats. He adorned the entire outfit with a shimmering, red cape that floated around him. His people had been very busy.

The media had captured one of the most iconic images in history – the first sighting of a true comic book super-hero.

Louis said nothing. He barely acknowledged the press below. He dropped quickly through the roof and into the fire.

The world watched as every station switched to the CCTV feed. The Rocket blew the fire away from the chlorine storage tanks before having three people wrap their arms tightly around his shoulder. He flew them through the hole in the roof and down to paramedics. The fire surged again by the time he flew back into the building. He seemed near panic as he looked across the one-hundred-and-thirty-four people still inside.

"Brilliant," I said to myself and shook my head. As always, he had thought nothing through. He just barged in playing the hero.

He raced to a nearby wall jabbing his meaty fingers into the metal lining there. He tore and dug until he had ripped through the steel exposing the brick beyond. One punch, and he'd cleared a hole through the brick large enough for the others to file out. With the last one through, he sped through the building confirming that no one else was left behind.

He emerged from the building to the cheers of everyone outside. He faked humility as he dropped his eyes to the ground and rubbed the back of his head in that aw shucks way only Louis Bryant could.

"That's a big hole," I said. The words had barely crossed my lips when the old brick structure gave way. The Rocket had destabilized the building. When it collapsed, chlorine mist exploded into the air. People screamed and scattered.

The Rocket panicked. He ran around the cloud of gas funneling as much of it as he could into the air. Four people died from inhaling chlorine. Seven fire fighters were injured and two died fighting the fire that spread through the warehouse district after the building collapse. At the end of it all, Louis gripped the side of a fire truck for support. He could barely stand.

And the fools on the ground cheered their incompetent hero.

Hall looked at Jordan and me. We were the only two people still in the governor's office. The others had been excused so we could watch the tragedy in private. "This is why we wait, Quinn," he pointed to the screen. "Had we gone after The Rocket, we'd have been sunk."

"Were you not watching the same thing I was?" I asked him.

"What are you talking about?" He looked back to the monitor as an EMS wrapped a blanket around The Rocket and he was walked to a nearby ambulance through a swarm of admirers cheering his every step. "He's a hero!"

"He's responsible for someone dying," I said. "Maybe more before the night is through."

"Responsible?" The governor was stunned. "Are you insane."

"Either he's responsible or you are," I stated firmly.

"He's right, Jeffery," Jordan spoke. We both looked at him. "Those people were going to die on national TV. Those systems weren't properly maintained. You and I know it. The left will jump all over this. Negligence. You could potentially face serious labor and safety violations."

Realization hit Hall.

"You had a plan," I assured. "We were about to bring down those barricades. We had overridden the controls and were about to send the command when The Rocket dropped a portion of the roof on the server room. Then, out of ignorance, he weakened the structure and was responsible for those people's deaths. And the destruction of private property."

Jordan added, "Herion's team will back up the hacking story. They were already trying to get in. I can get him to say they broke the codes but had no time to do anything. He'll be looking for cover here, too. I'm sure we can find a structural engineer or two to attest to him bringing down the building."

"I have the articles already out there. I can get a friendly reporter or two to amplify those in exchange for increased campaign access," I said.

Hall thought about it.

"Get in front of this or it'll steamroll you," I added.

Hall agreed.

***

As expected, Randall Wright, the democrat representative that replaced Jones, leaped onto the negligence story. But his camp waited a couple days to allow time for memorials and remembrances. He didn't want to be seen as politicizing the tragedy.

I left Hall's presidential campaign knowing I could be more effective on my own. I did the local press circuit. First responders had been harmed. Killed. Innocent lives were lost. I had the national news repeating calls to bring The Rocket to justice before Wright's camp ever mentioned corporate malfeasance. The system-override story was a matter of fact in the public eye.

Hall did his part. Once the story had national traction, he publicly requested his Attorney General open an investigation into The Rocket's criminal responsibility.

I authored a bill that classified enhanced persons with unnatural abilities as public utilities while using their powers. It gave our state the right to prosecute anyone crossing into our state and using their powers without permission. The ambiguous language made the law retroactive. That meant the state could bring charges against Louis Bryant. A few connections I made at Ivanwald ensured the legislature brought the bill to the floor quickly.

Public opinion moved to our side and the party recognized my work. It seemed our representative would be up for re-election just after I finish law school. They wanted my name on the ballot. I was married three months after passing the bar and campaigning for US Congress.

<u>Chapter Seven</u>

"My opponent has spent the last several weeks committing character assassination against a real, American hero to distract from the reality that corporate neglect and lack of public oversight was the real villain. He would have you blame The Rocket…" Representative Wright paused his debate closing statement for cheers from the crowd. Receiving only a little applause, he continued, "He would blame The Rocket to distract you from his father-in-law and mentor's complicity in the deaths of first responders. Mister Constance's party has been increasingly rabid about blaming a good citizen to distract the American public. My opponent is simply towing the party line. Voters deserve better than a young man who places party politics and power above his country."

I stepped from behind my podium replacing Representative Wright at center stage. We were three weeks from election day and less than one point separated us at the polls. No one thought it was possible. He was one of the most powerful men in Washington. Hall had convinced the state party to use my campaign to test the waters around my strategy. If I looked like I was making a dent in Wright's popularity, they'd consider incorporating it into the broader campaign.

As I expected, The Rocket controversy became a nationally polarizing issue with hard lines drawn between vapid hero-worship and liberty. My campaign was outperforming even my friendliest media pundit's predictions.

"In his first term, Representative Wright has rubber-stamped the radical agenda of one of the worst tax-and-spend administrations in recent history." Any real study of political history would point out that this wasn't remotely true, but this was politics. "This agenda includes the erasure of traditional values and the total decimation of states' rights. When a state cannot protect its people and its sovereignty from the invasion of those wielding unparalleled power, its People can no longer defend themselves or their private property from government overreach. We cannot be certain of an enhanced individual's political persuasion or loyalties. Preventing these individuals from using their powers to advance outside agendas against the will of the People is the right of every state.

"Mister Wright very clearly feels that the state should be allowed to ban firearms. The Rocket is far more powerful than any firearm.

"We have seen how irresponsible this administration has been with our military. What could they… what would they do with the help of a leftist super-hero?"

The applause I received at that dwarfed any Wright had gotten all night. My political upset became national news. Driving the nail into Wright's political coffin boosted every candidate aligned with me by three points or more.

The President addressed the nation in a primetime statement hoping to stop the coming storm. With his second term ending, he did everything he could to undermine our march toward liberty. His party tried forcing through legislation expanding the Civil Rights Act to include genetic mutation. They wanted to enshrine the rights of the enhanced to use their powers across state lines into law.

My strategy had made the enhanced a central election issue across the country. People feared the changing world. They were desperate for strength in the face of this sinister invasion.

I provided that strength.

My bill passed. We knew it would be challenged in the courts. But it ensured the opposition would remain on the defensive the entire campaign cycle. Before an injunction against enforcing the law was enacted by the state Supreme Court, Hall had The Rocket arrested. National media was on the scene as he surrendered himself to State Police.

Louis's state wouldn't extradite him. We all knew this. But I knew Louis. I knew he had to be the perfect little boy scout. He emulated the weakest characters.

I encouraged Hall to announce the arrest warrant at a press conference on the State House steps. Flanked by his Attorney General and State Police, Hall read the public endangerment and man slaughter charges. The Rocket appeared on stage no more than twenty seconds after Hall finished and surrendered himself. Thanks to the national media, everyone witnessed the handcuffs closing on his wrists. With head hanging in defeat, the police escorted him off stage and into the back seat of an unmarked SUV. He wasn't allowed a public statement.

I hadn't been there. I didn't want to be. This would be Hall's win even though I orchestrated the entire thing. For my efforts, the governor made sure I knew where The Rocket was going to be jailed.

I watched as Louis was booked. I can't describe the satisfaction I felt seeing the black stains on his hands after they took his fingerprints. I nearly laughed when he posed in his little costume for his mugshots. And I stood proudly in the lobby when they paraded him from booking to the empty wing of the state prison where he was to be locked away.

We locked eyes as he passed. I couldn't read his face. I don't know if he was just surprised to see me there or if he knew that I was responsible for his downfall. It didn't matter. His eyes lowered as the police walked him by.

The empty wing of the prison was my idea. I knew his strength and I knew the risks if he decided to stop being compliant. We could have a prison break on our hands if The Rocket walked through the cinderblock walls.

"I want to see him," I said to the Sherriff after Louis was safely in his cell.

"Yeah, yeah. Hall told me you two grew up together or something," she responded. "Still damned stupid to get into a cage with him. You get that, right?"

"He's not a threat. Not to me."

She rolled her eyes but walked me past the security check point and into the prison. She personally walked me to the doors of Louis's cell. Louis sat on the ragged cot there without looking at us. "Open it," she spoke into her shoulder-mounted microphone.

The electronic lock clanked, and the door slid open. I stepped into the cell and the door closed behind me.

"Good morning, Louis," I said.

"Why are you doing this, Quinn?" he responded.

"You good?" the Sherriff asked me again.

"I am. Thank you." She exited leaving Louis and I alone. "May I?" I pointed at the cot on the opposite cell wall. He stared. So, I sat.

"Why?"

"You're dangerous, Louis. You have always been dangerous. You killed a man on the field. And the factory…"

"Stop with the talking points. Why are you doing this?"

"You're the end of the human spirit," I stated. Clearly. Concisely. "You're the death of ingenuity. You're where American exceptionalism ends. Why would mere humans bother working toward a more perfect union when a supreme being walks among us?"

He sat silent staring stupidly at me.

"Have you not been paying attention to violent crime rates around the country?"

"What?"

"I guess when you're a god you don't have to pay attention to what's happening in the regular world."

"I'm not a…"

I interrupted his protest. "You wear a Mary Sue mask skipping your way through one challenge after another without noticing the destruction you leave in your wake. With super-heroes come super villains. Crime has been spiraling out of control. Murder rates are skyrocketing."

The stats spoke for themselves. Militias around the country were mobilizing and hunting the enhanced and anyone associated with them. And the enhanced were reciprocating the violence. Had he created his own Fortress of Solitude? Had he truly missed out on the world exploding into chaos?

"The new world you've created is one of death and destruction. You're a false god."

He sat silently before mustering the courage to

respond. "Do you seriously believe that crap, Quinn?"

"Who was the second-best pitcher in the state senior year, Louis?" I asked catching him off guard again.

"What?"

"The second-best pitcher in ninety-six," I pressed. "Who was it?"

He thought for a minute, but no name came to mind.

"No one remembers, Louis. No one even came close to touching your stats. In high school. In college. Football. Baseball. No one. Your competitors were passed over by scouts and for scholarships because everyone's eyes were only on The Rocket."

He looked confused. He never bothered to think about it. The room chilled when I spoke again.

"Were the people watching you or were they watching your powers?" I asked. He didn't answer. "You cause harm by simply existing."

I stood and walked to the door. Before I called for the guard, Louis spoke again. "What about you?"

I turned to him. "What about me?" I asked.

"Your intelligence. School was so easy for you. Perfect grades. Full scholarship. Top of your class. About to win a congressional seat. That seems unnatural, too."

"I worked for where I am," I barked. "I made the sacrifices."

"I sacrificed, too. I worked hard. I put everything I had into every game I played. I worked hard in school, too. I earned my grades. I wasn't as smart as you, so it was harder for me. But I earned my degree just like you did. And I worked at friendships."

"If that's what you call work," I sneered.

"You bailed on me. I reached out to you over and over, but you thought you were better than everyone else. Unlike you, I didn't close myself off." We sat in silence while I searched for words.

He spoke first. "I see your mom more often than you. Did you know that?" When I didn't respond, he continued, "I see her almost every week at the grocery store. I still load her bags in the car for her. Do you know how her hip surgery went last week?"

That one stung. I hadn't had a chance to call her with everything going on. I wanted to leap at him. Tear his face off. Beat him to a pulp. But my impulse control was impeccable.

"Quinn, you've only ever thought about yourself. You only ever surrounded yourself with people you could use. Everyone else was disposable."

"I have devoted my entire life to being better," I defended. "Better than the life I was born into. Better every day. And now that I am a better person, I hope to serve and to lead. To make the world a stronger, safer place. One guided by principles and not the whims of fringe ideologues or cultists."

"You have no idea what service is. It requires humility. It requires a desire to stand by your neighbor as you would yourself. I see you parading around with a Bible courting churches. If you bothered to ever read that book instead of just waiving it around like a flag, you'd know that Jesus washed the feet, not the face. True service lifts from the bottom. It protects the least among us. Your infatuation with power and status has made you lose sight of where you came from."

"Service takes strength," I responded. "You have that in abundance. That's how you can be so deluded. Humans cannot serve without power, and you always had power. I had to work for mine."

He glared incredulously. I hoped, somehow, I had wounded him.

I called for the guard. "Bye, Louis," I said before leaving in his cell.

He was only in prison for five hours before the court's injunction went into place and The Rocket was set free.

***

I beat Wright by three percentage points. Many others in my caucus won their elections also.

Hall wasn't as lucky.

The national vote was still behind The Rocket, so the sitting Vice President took the Presidency. We gained seats in the House and Senate. We remained the House minority but closed the gap. The Senate was an even split. The new Vice President would break ties in the administration's favor.

Hall's retirement from public life effectively ended the old guard within our party and seated me very influentially at the head of a strong new generation of thought. With Celeste and I married, Hall was still useful where I needed to finesse some of the more traditional party members.

The Supreme Court killed our bill, but our movement was only just beginning. Allies in other states worked new laws through hoping to prevent the unlicensed use of enhanced abilities. The new administration continued pressing for the adoption of the Enhanced Persons' Rights amendment to the Civil Rights Act, but we were killing almost every chance at negotiation on this. If we could get a state-centered action to stick before the opposition could pass a federal override, we stood a better chance.

In the meantime, the President took the push against sovereignty to the United Nations. More and more of the enhanced began creeping out of the shadows in the wake of The Rocket's celebrity status.

The European Union had already passed a law allowing enhanced people to move freely throughout all member nations. Most of theirs were acting as extensions of emergency response and medical services. There were plenty of success stories, but some questionable violations of religious medical exemptions.

A Muslim girl in France needed a new kidney. Compatible donors were extremely rare, but they found a willing Jew in Germany who was a match. The girl's health began to fail rapidly, and they were losing their window for a safe transplant. Rather than losing time bringing the man to France, they decided to extract his kidney in Germany and have a speedster out of Poland race it to Paris for an emergency procedure.

The speedster was a kid who could run more than twelve hundred miles per hour. The procedures went flawlessly. The little Muslim girl lived. Everyone was happy.

Except for the girl's family.

As happy as they were to still have their daughter, they were Palestinian immigrants. The thought of their daughter with a Jewish kidney cloaked their entire family in religious shame. The family was shunned from their mosque. Their home was vandalized. The father lost his job. Ultimately, once the daughter was home, she was abused and blamed for the family's misfortunes.

An online campaign raised money for her to emancipate herself from her parents and move to the UK. That never happened. The entire incident was horrible to watch. Had the hospital operated within the proper channels… had the family's wishes not been ignored… had a speedster not believed their "help" didn't require parental input or the permission of the governments whose borders they violated, perhaps that little girl would still be here today.

Four very powerful enhanced individuals in Russia were rumored to be extensions of the Kremlin. Their "vigilante activity" seemed to directly align with domestic security forces, and NATO feared what would happen if they were added to the Russian military.

Still, The U.N. Security Council took up the matter of the free movement of enhanced citizens across member-state borders with proper licensing. This move was championed by the US, Israel, Great Britain, Russia, and China.

I spoke out vehemently against this. The U.N. was further erasing the sovereignty of nations. And I had my followers.

The mainstream media focused on one positive story after another. Kittens were rescued from trees. Shop lifters were held for the police. A suicide had been prevented.

After his release, The Rocket continued his super-hero cosplay. He assisted Border Patrol in dismantling an international human trafficking network. National news programing couldn't get enough of these feel-good stories.

But they weren't covering the other side of it. Vigilantes were stopping minor crimes and people were getting hurt.

In Nevada, a woman had been getting gas when some teenagers attempted to carjack an old man two pumps over. The woman could sling fire from her fingertips. This unfolded as expected. The car being jacked tore away pulling the pump line with it. The woman shot tendrils of flames trying to block their escape, but only succeeded in igniting the car, the tank, and the entire convenience station. Everyone died; fifteen people including the teenagers, the old man, the woman, and her two children.

I had begun spending my days away from Congress speaking at rallies and conventions around the country. Unlike my peers, I gave little to no time to the hundreds of lobbyists requesting my time. I was heralding an uprising.

One night after a speech I gave at San Diego Christian College, my cellphone rang. Bale Akello was on the other end when I answered. His father had been assassinated the month before in an attempted military coup. He had befriended several enhanced people and they helped him retake control and execute the coup leaders. He hoped to persuade me of the value of the enhanced.

"Bale," I said. "It is so good to hear your voice and I am thrilled to see you reclaim your birthright even though it was because of such horrific events. You showed a true strength in reclaiming your nation. I can only hope to do for my nation what you are doing for yours.

"But your people understand their place in the divine order. We coddle our weak. We pretend the infirm are worthy and that equality is a virtue. We spare the rod. Your enhanced serve. Ours would dominate."

Our conversation volleyed between the personal and matters of State. In the end, he agreed to keep an open mind and continue to hear me out. Before we ended our call, we prayed together.

***

Celeste and I were married for nearly two years by that time. Ours had been a large ceremony. I didn't care much for the tradition, but Celeste was Jeffrey's princess and he ensured she'd have her dream wedding. He even covered our post-election honeymoon to Fiji. As relaxing as the trip had been, and as much as Celeste desperately tried to convince me that I had earned the break, all I wanted was to get to DC and get to work. I had never been one to sit back and let life just happen to me.

Our college courtship had been very public. Hall was popular. Very popular. He was only a handful of electoral college votes away from winning the Presidency. I tried to convince him that he would have dominated had he just listened to me. He disagreed.

While Celeste and I lived together a few years, we were very public about our reasons for not marrying earlier. In fact, had I not been thrust onto the campaign trail, we would have waited longer. No matter my message, us not being married was seen as a negative in the polls. Early campaign ads attacked my character as if I was unable to commit. Hence, the almost royal wedding followed by victory followed by vacation ultimately ending in my beautiful bride standing beside me as I was sworn into office.

Between my Congressional responsibilities, speaking engagements, and meetings, Celeste and I rarely saw each other. We mostly spent time together on the few weekends we could escape to the Hall family lake house. Her parents spent more and more time there since his public career was virtually over.

She worked hard to become an artist while I was in law school. She found a place in the local art community and built a network of friends. Her work was shown in a few shows with other artists. But her first solo show flopped. Unfortunately, I wasn't there. Budget negotiations were tense and most of my evenings were spent in dinners and sleeping on the sofa in my office.

She did let me preview her pieces. There were twenty-three paintings and seven sculptures celebrating heroism. She had talent. There were a few pieces in there I didn't care for. With the rise of the enhanced around the nation, of course those concepts were present in her work. She didn't like it when I said it felt like she was undermining me publicly through this show.

That was our first big fight. Lots of shouting.

In the end, her show went nowhere, and she threw in the towel. She began her teaching career at a nearby private elementary school.

She stayed active in the art scene. Celeste planned shows for other artists and brought some of them into her art class as guest speakers. The kids loved her. She quickly became the favorite teacher and a socialite representative's wife.

When my speaking engagements morphed into a rally tour after my second year in Congress, we saw each other even less. She would fly out to meet me at a rally or two every few weeks, but she mostly stayed home.

***

"Oh, you're home," Celeste said when she walked into the kitchen after work to find me there. "I wasn't sure you'd be here this weekend."

We had spoken earlier that week. The Houston rally was huge. One of the biggest so far. That was Tuesday. By Wednesday evening, I was in DC voting against a bill that would allow local, state, and federal law enforcement to deputize the enhanced. It was an abomination of a bill.

There was an ongoing civil suit in Wyoming against the F.B.I. after a botched raid on a survivalist compound. Almost immediately after The Rocket went public, more and more of the enhanced were coming out of the woodwork. A bulletproof seventeen-year-old had joined an early police training program. Because he was invulnerable, he'd been allowed on several S.W.A.T. raids already, but the feds raiding the compound over some land dispute was too good for the kid to sit out.

Negotiations went nowhere. The kid convinced the senior agent on site to let him go in and bring them out. Everyone was glued to the national news as the kid walked straight for the ranch house. Glasses broke and the people inside began shooting. Bullets bounced off the kid as he kicked in the door and dragged the leader out by his collar. The guy shot at the kid until his gun was empty. The kid just smiled.

Then the cameras turned toward the civilian crowd that had gathered to watch the commotion. Six had taken a bullet that had bounced off the kid. Two people died. Four more were in critical condition for more than three weeks.

The operation was cleared of negligence following an internal investigation. The kid should never have been allowed to go in. It was an irresponsible move. The administration's reaction to this was to push a bill legalizing this travesty. The injured and the families brought a civil suit.

After days of meetings and lobbying, we narrowly defeated the bill. I called it a week and went home.

"I am," I answered Celeste. "This is our lake weekend, right?"

She rolled her eyes. "Did you not get my message? I'm curating a show tomorrow evening. I can't go."

I needed to talk to Jeffery. The party wasn't coalescing around me. We were going to hand the liberals a fourth consecutive term if we didn't start fighting. I needed Hall out of retirement and standing with me.

"Couldn't someone else do that for you?"

"No, Quinn," she bluntly spoke. "I can't. I'm responsible for this show. Andre is…"

"Andre Whitehurst?" I asked knowing the name. Of course. Andre was a rising star throughout the region, and he'd taken a special liking to Celeste. He was the one who convinced her to have that solo show. He had a prestigious gallery and offered her the space.

"Of course," she grumbled. "I've been organizing shows at his gallery for months."

I stood. "I still need to talk to your father," I said.

"Of course, you do," she responded.

I started to leave the kitchen when she spoke again. "I want a divorce." Her voice broke when she said it. "I can't keep going like this."

I turned back to her. She looked at the floor as if her statement was the darkest confession. I looked back at her with a benevolent smile. Forgiving.

"I know about you and Andre," I said. Her eyes met mine. She was terrified. "I've always known." I suspected, but I could somehow read her soul in that instance. My mind instantly replayed our every interaction. Andre taught at the local design school. She met him the first year after moving back from Parsons. I heard the giggles. I read the gazes. The shame when they desperately tried to not make eye contact while I was around. She said I changed too much, that I was no longer the man she had fallen in love with. But I knew her attraction to power superseded her desire for romance.

Still, I wasn't there. I was an absentee king away from his castle. Celeste couldn't be faulted for carrying on an affair with Andre. And Celeste's playtime was no threat to me.

"No," I said. Her fear dissolved into confusion.

"No?" She asked.

"No divorce. We're fine."

Her jaw fell. "But..."

"If I cared about your love life, I'd have said so before now. We have been beneficial to one another. I see no reason for that to change," I said.

"I just told you that I don't love you anymore," she said.

"That stopped being a factor years ago," I said. "Our individual goals are being met. I see no reason for that to change. Keep your little affair. Just keep it private. Your standard of living needn't suffer."

She was silent. Stunned. I could see that she hadn't expected the night to go this way.

I hugged her and kissed her on her forehead. It was cold… without affection. But it was somehow comforting to us both.

I went upstairs and packed my bags for the marathon of travel I had ahead of me.

***

Hall was surprised to see me three hours later at the lake house. Celeste had told him about Andre already and prepared him for the news. She had been trained from an early age to be open with personal matters for the good of the family.

She hadn't told him about our conversation, however. Maybe she just didn't know how to explain it to him. He assumed I would be packing my things and moving out.

He was having a drink on the porch when I ascended the steps to the lake house. I sat with him after getting a bottle of water out of the refrigerator and I brought him up to speed on Celeste's and my agreement. He fumed in silence until I brought up the party. The old guard was lethargic. Ineffective. They had no direction and were being drug along by the opposition. My caucus had a clear message.

When the legal efforts against The Rocket ultimately failed, the E.P.A. began looking into the failed containment at the chemical plant. His business assets had been frozen as a part of the investigation. As such, Hall was increasingly convinced the structural damage caused by The Rocket had been responsible for the equipment failure. He had grown more and more fervently anti-enhanced.

I proposed a campaign that would stop this administration at one term. Our destiny was to lead. We needed to secure the sanctity and dominion of the human against the fascist tide of the super-human. I had a winning strategy.

Jefferey wasn't convinced. He knew I could win, but he had too much baggage with the potential criminal investigation.

I told him what the government had wouldn't hold up. It was a political witch hunt. I told him I could kill the investigation. When he doubted me, I convinced him to give me a month.

***

First thing that Monday morning, I sat in Bale Akello's office at the United Nations.

He greeted me with a tight hug. We talked of our days at Ivanwald and caught up on each other's lives. He had cleared his morning to sit with me.

Bale and I spoke often in the few weeks after our San Diego phone conversation. After he stood strong in the face of a military coup and won the security of his nation, UN member-states wanted to hear his thoughts on the proposal to allow the enhanced to cross national borders for emergency response.

Bale used the enhanced to secure his country and initially believed the proposal to be a good thing. I convinced him of the inherent dangers. The resolution would create a protected class that stood above the general population that could operate without oversight despite the will of the People. In essence, every nation would be subject to unmatched foreign operatives moving freely throughout their territory.

"But this limits their movement to times of crisis," Bale argued. "Is it not general custom to allow refugees to freely cross borders and request amnesty?"

"Refugees still have to get permission to enter a country," I answered. "Would the enhanced be forced to obey the laws and traditions of the countries they invaded? Would they be bound by any laws? Would they swear loyalty to that nation's leadership, or would they unilaterally act against rightful leaders? What would their unregulated agenda be?"

Bale pondered this.

"Imagine what happens when a faction not aligned with you receives assistance from enhanced state operatives who bring your palace down around you before your first alarms sound."

Ultimately, I convinced him of the threat. His international notoriety presented an opportunity. Bale requested time to speak on the issue of the enhanced. I slipped word to the Saudis about Bale's topic. I knew a few people in the royal court who wanted nothing more than defeating this proposition. They spread word to sympathetic member states, and we quickly had a large, online buzz around Bale's speech.

A member of Congress secretly negotiating with other nations against the current administration is explicitly illegal, but the ends justified the means. I was protecting the world from itself.

We spent that Monday in his office polishing his speech. His delivery was eloquent. Strong. Authoritative. More than a few ambassadors who formally supported the resolution stood in applause.

***

We defeated the Enhanced Person's Emergency Authority Resolution. The thought of enhanced supremacy resonated with the international community.

Ivanwald members watched the rise of the enhanced with caution. Many felt that the enhanced represented a historic threat unlike anything humanity has ever seen, but they weren't sure exactly how to handle the threat. Religious leaders remained as neutral as they could while hinting that the enhanced could be God's chosen. But most of the messaging had been tempered with the reality that no one wanted to preemptively assign a divine purpose to these beings if they decided to enslave the rest of humanity.

Leadership hoped we could bring some of the more high-profile enhanced into the Ivanwald fold. They thought if they could bring them into the fold and use them to correct the global scales of power, we could right the world. Their obvious first choice had been The Rocket.

For clear reasons, I had been kept at a distance while they courted Louis. But my allies within the organization reported that ill-fated attempt. Long before we arrested The Rocket, Liberty University President Ronald Provist, Pastor Angelica West out of Fort Worth, and Colorado Senator Lincoln Grayson were sent to court The Rocket. He greeted them personally and invited them into his home, but they were forced into a hurried exit after trying to minister to him. News vans were almost permanently camped around his house at that time, and they caught the trio fast-stepping to their limo with Louis calling them frauds and false prophets at the top of his lungs on camera.

After that, Ivanwald was only able to coax the most fringe into our fold, but we kept them out of the public eye until we could agree about what to do with them. With Bale's speech at the UN, our new course was set.

We immediately stopped courting the enhanced. Those already among our ranks were dealt with. If they couldn't be handled directly, they were paid handsomely to disappear.

Ministries with ties to Ivanwald began warning of the dangers presented by the enhanced. Churches not directly associated with Ivanwald still purchased their sermons and lesson plans from Ivanwald-linked religious publishers. They increasingly spoke of demonic influence ushering in the end of days.

My phone rang the morning after Bale's speech. Hall wanted to hear my suggestions. The government's case was falling apart around them. New pressures from select people I knew in the Justice Department quietly moved the case against Hall on the back burner.

"These aren't suggestions, Jeffrey. I'm managing the campaign. I make the calls. Policy and messaging are mine. When you're in office, I'm your Chief Strategist."

"Chief Strategist!" he scoffed.

"That's the deal. If you had listened to me last campaign, you'd be sitting in the Oval Office right now."

Silence. Then, "Can I think about this?"

"You have two days. I'm hitting the mid-morning news cycle with or without you." I had lined up O'Banyoun and Roche as fallbacks if I couldn't secure Hall. But Hall had been beaten. Broken. He was ripe for this.

Every morning show carried "exclusive" interviews with Hall. By the evening, he was dominating the national news. His message was clear: the United States has been made a laughingstock in the President's misguided attempt to set the enhanced above the laws of man and God.

Hall joined my rally tour a year and a half before primary season. By the time the primaries rolled around, he had no serious competition. And, though the incumbent won the popular vote, Hall's Electoral College victory was decisive.

I had crowned the most powerful man on Earth.

<u>Chapter Eight</u>

With Hall's candidacy, the rest of the party fell in line. We took both houses of Congress and the White House.

When The Rocket first came out, the public was enthralled. Merchandising flew off the shelves. As more and more of the enhanced suited up, kids picked their favorites and games like Cops and Robbers changed into Heroes and Villains. It was as if the Second Coming happened, and Christ was a rockstar.

By the time Hall sat behind the Oval Office desk, the public was usefully afraid. Their idol worship quickly morphed into a righteous fear of emerging demonic forces. Everyday people began to stand their ground.

There was a shrinking man in Wisconsin. He spent a couple years working with emergency services. Mostly, he did anti-drug school assemblies in costume and some fire safety awareness videos for several fire departments around the state. There were rumors that he'd helped shut down an active shooter in Appleton high school, but he never admitted to it.

A factory worker in Milwaukee saw him outside his twelve-year-old daughter's bedroom window and shot him. It was a million-to-one shot because the guy was about the size of a beetle at the time. That story became a favorite at our rallies that first year. An enhanced peeping pedophile killed by a father protecting his child played well nearly everywhere we went.

We dropped the story from our greatest hits after it came out that the father was sexually abusing that little girl. Apparently, the building's doorman knew the beetle guy and tipped him off to his suspicions about the father. We buried the abuse revelation.

Hall's administration sat more judges than any other in U.S. history. Through Hall, I reshaped the face of American law while introducing legislation against the enhanced at both the national and the state level. I strengthened State's Rights to regulate what the enhanced could do within their borders.

Of course, the snowflakes challenged these laws in court. They pretended we were somehow denying them civil rights when we limited their ability to threaten the very nature of humanity. It was shameful really. Cowardice. Weakness. The court system tied up their time and money while we leveraged national resources against them. Our judges dismissed every case possible and delayed those they couldn't.

Insulating herself from the political grindhouse, Celeste moved to Seattle with Andre and lived under the radar. I sold the house and moved into a penthouse within blocks of the White House. Two floors beneath me were dedicated to NSA operatives and the Secret Service. My protection was an extension of the President's detail. Hall and I became interchangeable.

Throughout the first two years of his administration, I had Hall booked at two or three rallies around the country and no less than four call-in interviews with rightwing news outlets each month. He told me it was worse than the regular campaign trail. But we owned the news cycle every day. Enhanced-rights loons sounded more like the whining children they are than any viable opposition. The left was fractured.

Of course, I recognize the farce in such a statement. Within the political spectrum, the American "left" was just right of center. But the general rabble, couldn't process the concept. To them, there was only good and evil. God or the Devil. Nuance has no place in authoritarianism. If you're not with us, you're against us. And we were the People of the United States.

Where would that leave those standing against us?

It left them broken. They were lost in identity politics debating among themselves what type of person they would support and which they would abandon to the smokehouses. They ignored the real threat of the god race walking amongst us.

Weakness infiltrated the United Nations over its decades of existence. False neutrality and bureaucracy crippled the international organization turning it into a quagmire of inaction. Our administration changed that. The strength and resolve of humanity would once again stand as a testament that rogue nations would no longer be tolerated. We worked tirelessly to ensure the UN, formed originally to prevent the rise of another global totalitarian threat, would not lose site of its original mandate. Unlike the threat of foolish men who thought they were superior to others based on skin color or nationality, the new threat the UN faced was one to the continued existence of humanity as represented by an emerging species… the enhanced. I was determined to secure the future for humanity. Redirecting the UN took a lot of work.

Every morning for the first six months of Hall's presidency, I would sit with him for security briefings. We would set his daily agenda and review talking points for whatever meetings or rallies we had scheduled. Then I would meet with Bale and a growing group of international representatives for the greater work.

We initially focused on building an alliance of nations. Bale's speech defeated a single resolution, but there was a lot of public support for enhanced supremacy. We needed a coalition of powerful countries who could organize against this troublesome trend.

To achieve this, we first sought our old enemies. Iran. Syria. North Korea. Vietnam. China. With Ugandan support, we locked in most of the potential African Union nations. All we had to promise them was to end our ludicrously ineffective sanctions regime and deliver more national autonomy.

Hall almost blew a gasket when I reached out to Russia. "What the hell do you mean you contacted the Kremlin? You're treading treason waters, Quinn," he snapped.

"I know it sounds counter-intuitive, Jeffrey," I calmed.

"Counter intuitive? It sounds insane."

"The United States has cuddled up to the softest, most bureaucratically paralyzed nation-states around the world. They're fat. Wealthy."

"They're wealthy because they won, Quinn. They're the leaders of the free world."

"They cling to dying ideologies and are strangled by old money. None of them can make a decision without the input of shadowy corporate heads too comfortable with their wealth to make the necessary changes."

"Those corporate heads are our donors."

"Where will their wealth be when a bleeding heart with powers like The Rocket decides to redistribute their wealth and end global poverty? Where will it be when fights between the enhanced eradicate national borders and infrastructure?

"We ran on a platform of keeping these monsters in check. We have a mandate from the People, Jeffrey. We can't fulfill our campaign promises if the UN allows these people to destroy our national sovereignty."

His face flushed red. "It's Mr. President, if you don't mind."

I smiled. He had nothing and was clamoring for tradition. "Fine, Mr. President. I'm your Chief Strategist and if you want to keep that fancy little title, you're going to listen to me."

He seethed, but he said nothing.

I explained to him the need for former enemies. Russia knew how much damage the U.S. could cause. We could decimate their economy. We could shut down their every point of access to the shipping channels throughout the Mediterranean and China Seas limiting them to either land or frozen northern routes for transport. And we could do all of this without a single direct action. Our strategic dominance collapsed them in the Cold War, and we were much stronger today.

And they knew that we paled in might compared to an organized group of the enhanced.

We were offering something no administration before us could offer; a stronger position in the U.S.-dominated global economy and a position as an equal in what I called the "Brotherhood of Nations."

We dismantled the brinksmanship remnants of the Cold War and replaced it with a system of honor and loyalty. We silently backed out of NATO and Russia was able to bring in many of the former Soviet bloc nations by signing the Brotherhood's treaty of non-interventionism. Each member state would be allowed pure sovereignty on all domestic matters and mutual military assistance in the event of illegal enhanced activity.

Because we held both chambers of Congress, ratifying the new treaties was a cake walk.

Within a year, presidents, prime ministers, monarchs, despots, and warlords crossed sabers and swore to the Brotherhood. Alongside Russia and China, we ensured UN membership for all Brotherhood states. Any concept of the free international movement of the enhanced became an impossibility.

After the first two years of his administration, Hall's health began to catch up with him. I had him on a rock star's schedule. He wasn't a healthy man going into his first term, and the stress of the feverish schedule caught up to him.

He had a minor heart attack.

We kept it out of the news. While it barely slowed him down, it did shock him. He couldn't maintain the same pace as he used to.

I took the lead at rallies and on the interview circuit. I spoke for the President. There were times when he objected to how I said things… especially when I started referring to enhancements as mutations and floated the question of whether they could even be considered human. Ultimately, he accepted my lead. I was right. He fell in line.

***

President Hall overwhelmingly won a second term. The election took place six weeks after the United Nations banned travel for the enhanced across national borders without the signed permission of the leadership of all bordering nations. We were free to secure our borders.

Thirty-four states are required to call a Convention of States. At the beginning of Hall's first term, nineteen states had requested one. By the end of that term, we had thirty-two. The liberal states were wanting to use the convention to codify liberal social garbage into the Constitution: equal rights, healthcare, the New Deal. That junk was popular, but endlessly debatable. The conservative states wanted to make States' Rights and commerce sacred.

The last two held out until the general election. Once Hall trounced his opponent, they passed convention resolutions. And, with that, the heart of American law was open for debate.

Thirty-eight states are required to ratify constitutional amendments. The problem for the left was that there are more rural states than densely populated ones. When each State gets one vote, empty land rules. The will of the People is easily amended.

And it was.

Ultimately, an equal rights amendment was added, but the wording was hollow and unenforceable. I made sure enhanced mutations were explicitly exempt from constitutional equal rights language.

We managed to get a citizenship definition amendment limiting citizenship rights to all humans natural-born, naturalized, or granted asylum. Fairly bland words. No one fully understood their strength. The people got their feel-good win. We didn't limit how the federal government granted or refused asylum. We even extended a type of citizenship to refugees. But we did limit citizenship to humans.

The bloodwork The Rocket submitted himself to those first few weeks after he changed the world was extensive. They tested his anti-viral capabilities. They studied the resiliency of his white blood cells. They did bone density tests. I believe they even took a sample of his brain matter. They ran several rounds of these tests taking samples over the course of about three months until the needles would no longer pierce his skin.

For the next few years, they studied his samples they had alongside other samples taken from other enhanced individuals. They found the enhanced were developing increased immune density were increasing daily. Of course, The Rocket was leaps and bounds beyond the other enhanced people, but they all showed signs of increased virility and invulnerability.

I reached out to Rodger Husk, a geneticist whose brother-in-law I met at an Ivanwald social event. Rodger had been intrigued with The Rocket ever since he went public, but his lab had no ties to the NFL nor did they receive any government funding. This meant that he never got access to the samples. I pulled a few strings and got the Husk Lab a four-hundred-million-dollar private grant and access so that he could map enhanced DNA. What he found was astounding.

The human genome is composed of forty-six DNA molecules of twenty-four types. They're organized in identical pairs. The complexity of a human is generated by only three billion nucleotide pairs. It sounds like a lot, but the Australian lungfish has forty-three billion base pairs.

In the grand scheme, we're not that complicated.

The enhanced had twenty-five types of DNA molecules. It should have been impossible, but their DNA seemed to break down somewhere in their adolescent years. Once a few pairs split, they would reconstitute into pairs and begin resequencing the structure. Genetically, they were generating junk DNA that was mutating them.

Once we were able to legally categorize the enhanced as mutations, their citizenship was up for grabs.

Seventeen states and the US Congress passed bills stripping the enhanced of their American citizenship. But we didn't do this without compassion. If they registered with the federal government, they would maintain the civil rights associated with legal alien status.

They were given one year to register with the new Department of the Enhanced. Registration also meant any use of the enhanced person's power would be a felony punishable by forty years in federal prison. The death penalty would be invoked for violations resulting in a citizen's death.

After the first year, unregistered enhanced persons within the United States would be detained indefinitely.

Similar policies were enacted across Brotherhood nations.

In Russia, the enhanced were required to sign loyalty statements to the Kremlin or they were immediately executed. The Saudis purged the enhanced from their kingdom in the most Saudi way possible.

The enhanced rebelled in South Africa. They sat a new government with the strongest among them as dictator. He requested Brotherhood membership. Deliberation among Brotherhood nations was robust. The Israeli ambassador argued that accepting them would compromise our integrity, but I pointed out that our treaty guaranteed national sovereignty and refused cross-border operations of the enhanced. If South Africa was willing to agree to these terms and keep their activity within their own borders, there was no reason to deny their membership.

"Think of it as mutually guaranteed protection," I said. "So long as they keep the violence in their own house, we could use them as allies."

Most of the enhanced went underground. They stopped interfering in human lives. Humans were allowed to become self-sufficient again. People stopped relying on these anti-Christ figures for salvation.

There were some who continued to operate. Enhanced vigilantes and their super-criminal counterparts battled in the streets of liberal states. These states passed laws enshrining enhanced citizenship despite federal law. Hall felt this was a direct rejection of his administration and the rule of law. He wanted to send the FBI in against state orders.

I disagreed. "They're confined to those states, Jeffery. Let them stay there. Any move on our part to upend their twisted laws would only result in violence, and I'm sure that would escalate into something we're not yet prepared to handle. We should accept this compromise... for now."

The Rocket operated throughout the southeast. His family moved to the west coast during what was being called the Great Realignment. We wanted him arrested, but he was doing enough good, saving enough lives, that every cop encountering him somehow failed to take him into custody. With their body cameras turned off in every interaction with him, we had only their word that The Rocket resisted.

***

One of the other things we managed to do during the Constitution of States was to remove presidential term limits. The will of the People must not be infringed, after all. I needed Hall to hold the White House for one more term before I could run for office myself.

He wasn't in the best health and Kremp, his Vice President, was secretly suffering from early on-set dementia. Sure, I held the party in my hand and had my choice of new candidates, but I had no interest in waiting eight more years for my birthright. So, we kept Hall out of live events. When he spoke, it was on video on a controlled stage where we could make him seem virile. I handled most of his live events introducing pre-recorded speeches. The hordes of fans barely noticed. They wanted our ideas. The vessels delivering them were interchangeable.

The opposition lobbed another softball candidate our way. Their candidate… I barely remember his name at this point… tried making the election about the economy. With all our new trade partners, the economy was booming. The stock market was at historic highs. Prices fell. This is easy when your trade partners are borderline slaver nations. Of course, expanded global trade means a critical drop in the job market, but that just made for a boom for business expansion. With everyone begging for work meant that people were grabbing up three and four part time positions. The nation's productivity and profitability surged.

Mainstream media pundits called Hall a fascist without using those exact words. They tried linking our efforts to secure public safety from enhanced supremacy with Nazi Germany. They failed in their misinformation campaign. The reality was that they were as scared as everyone. Not even they believed the lies they spewed. The public's eyes were finally opened to the threat of human obsolescence.

Most people look at a prison and all they see is a prison… a collection of cells. They see a building. I see the components. A cage is a collection of hundreds of useless objects that, in and of themselves, do nothing to hold an animal. A bar is useful when you need to bludgeon something, but collect them into a grid, and we get an entrapment structure. A door, by its nature, is designed to open one area into another. Add a door to a cage, and it becomes part of the whole… a system from which there is little to no escape.

In one administration, we built a society that functioned systemically limiting the advancement of the enhanced and protecting the people from their would-be enslavers.

While we had no real political resistance, we did face growing unrest. It began with the death of Walter Greycar. He was seventeen and a drug dealer operating out of his mother's Section 8 apartment just outside Seattle, Washington. The Seattle Police Department patrolled that development twice a week openly stopping and frisking anyone standing around outside. Walter had been busted with twenty-eight grams of crack in a brown paper envelope. He claimed he was delivering it for someone and didn't know what was in it. The officers didn't believe him and took him into custody.

With HUD's zero-tolerance policy on criminal activity, the day after he was charged, his mother was issued a thirty-day notice of eviction. Her housing vouchers were canceled.

Walter's situation was common. This would have been a non-story, but Walter was enhanced. His body generated an electrical current. It began when he was six. He enjoyed popping his friends and family with static electricity. While it was strange that he could do that without rubbing his feet against carpet, no one thought it weird until he threw a lightning bolt from his fingertips after his sixteenth birthday.

The cops taunted Walter that first night. They wanted to know who he was transporting for. They said what they needed to get the kid to slip up. Some reporter got her hands on the interrogation video and released it to the public. The interrogating officer told Walter he'd turned his own mother into a homeless crack whore. Crude language. The cop stupidly used tried and true tactics on a new kind of criminal.

Walter got mad.

He blew a hole through the wall and escaped. The police found him exactly where they expected. He had gone home to his mother. It was a standoff… twelve cops aimed their guns at a scared an angry teenager. Cell phones galore recorded every angle. Electric current sparked around him lifting him a few inches off the ground. He charged for a massive blast. The cops fired.

When someone is a living weapon, lethal force is always justified. Agitators seized the moment. Almost on cue, protests broke out around the country. Hall and his cadre of idiots believed organizers were shipping in paid protestors, but I knew better. Still, them spreading nonsense created enough doubt that the potential uprising was de-legitimized and was stopped after a few easily dispersed riots.

Ultimately, public opinion went our way.

***

With the national borders secured and the Brotherhood of Nations agreement stronger than ever, our national politics focused entirely on domestic matters. We played identity-politics badminton while the wealthy and powerful of the Brotherhood continued their divine rule.

Israel got restless.

They weren't happy about the expansion limitations we demanded. Israel demanded to be wholly sovereign and able to secure its borders by expelling or exterminating Palestinians. The Brotherhood ensured Israel's borders included Jerusalem, but we required they stop further expansion into Gaza.

We were establishing a new world order of nationalistic self-determination. That required border disputes to be arbitrated. It also meant Israel and the newly formed Palestine would have defined borders. It was a two-state solution that no one really liked. In my opinion, that made it a good compromise. I didn't have the patience for land squabbles.

With our campaign in full swing, Israel did what we forbade them from doing. They moved their military into Abu Dis on Palestine's side of the border and established what they called an army settlement. Jerusalem's population exploded once the Brotherhood nations moved their embassies there. Instead of moving their people to less-populated areas within Israel, the administration played their typical hand expanding deeper into Palestinian territory.

There were countries that rejected Brotherhood membership. Germany. Cuba. Iceland. Remaining out of the Brotherhood invited international isolation. No access to major international trade markets. Limited international travel. Each of these nations were forced to eek out a borderline third world existence. Their people suffered because of their leaders' obsolescence. Still, a few of them maintained their UN membership.

The Cuban ambassador spoke out against the Israeli expansion. He asked the security council to intervene. He had to know that we wouldn't allow a vote against Israel. The US alone could veto any motion to sanction Israel, but Russia, China, and the UK were all standing members with the same power. The Cuban wasted his breath.

Publicly, the Brotherhood remained neutral. The invasion was an initiation of territorial negotiations between two sovereign nations and the international community had no place in those negotiations. The United Nations' uselessness was on display for the world to see.

Internally, the invasion was an annoyance. Hall's administration was forced to play global citizen thanks to unauthorized, unilateral actions by a Brotherhood state. It became harder to control the narrative. The wave of riots organized into and anti-fascist insurgency that began to resonate with the public.

Israel messed us up.

What Israel failed to see… what none of us saw coming… was a conflict with the enhanced.

***

A few weeks ago, I was resting at home. We had just spent the evening doing last minute debate prep with Hall. We had to inject him with stimulants to get him through the night. He'd need another dose before the debate. Each shot took twenty years off his brain.

I had an early morning ahead and had to pop a pill to get to sleep. Maybe I would join Hall for one of those stimulant shots in the morning. I hated the drugs. The sleep was unnatural and detached me too much from my mind. It was why I swore off alcohol.

But the ends here were justified.

When the sleep hit, it hit hard.

I awoke in a dream on the campaign trail. But it wasn't Hall's campaign trail. It was mine.

A nation of people gyrated at my feet. They were strong against a crumbling world, and I was their protector.

The throngs swayed and melted and were then smoke… circling… spiraling… reaching for God.

The smoke climbed into the air and fell back to earth as snow. Quickly, the sky filled with rising smoke and falling snow and my campaign banners were brilliant reds and whites and blues against the gray. I was hope.

I was warm.

The snow was warm.

The snow wasn't snow.

The snow was ash.

The people, my people, were smoke… were ash… were lost to the wind.

As I looked to the sun, hidden behind clouds of flakes, a black figure stood in the sky.

I knew who it was even though I couldn't see him clearly.

Louis Bryant.

***

The third and final debate of the campaign had just stopped when national security entered the stage and shut it down. Hall and I were whisked out of the building and to the Beast; the nearly indestructible limousine used to transport the president.

Israel's settlement was three weeks old. Armed resistance by the Palestinians had been steady, but ineffective. Five hours before the debate, three enhanced Palestinians landed in Jerusalem. The Israeli military met them with severe brutality. And they did it in front of news cameras.

The world was stunned.

The Brotherhood needed leadership. We stood by Israel's decision to expand even though it violated our agreement, and Israel had just murdered three enhanced Palestinians standing idly on the streets of Jerusalem. Detractors spoke up publicly.

The already volatile streets of the United States erupted in massive protests insisting the administration move to stop the violence.

"We can't do that, Quinn," Hall said as we walked into the Oval Office. "We can't have our governors move the National Guard into other states to quell this violence." I had suggested the plan in the limo on the way back to the residence. "It would tear the union apart."

"Riots in the street are tearing the nation apart, Jeffrey. These liberal governors who are letting rioters tear their cities to shreds while doing little to nothing to stop it are abandoning law and order to make you look week."

170

"Local and state police are out in force. It's all over the news. We can't..."

"We can and we will. Every step of the way, these governors have refused our offerings of military equipment and training while they skipped through the daisies hand in hand with the enhanced. They've let their people become unruly. Now, the world is burning around them.

"You're going on television in fifteen minutes telling the nation that these weak governors are going to accept the National Guard from other states, or we will move the US Army in to end this violence.

"And you're going to tell them that the act of these enhanced people illegally crossing into Israel's territory was a direct threat. Israel was justified in defending themselves."

"What were you watching, Quinn? The Palestinians knew what would happen to them. They wanted the world to see that horror show. They have the upper hand."

I backhanded him.

Hall's Secret Service detail moved forward, but I held up a hand and they dumbly stopped.

"That is one of the stupidest things I've ever heard come out of your mouth. Get a grip." I looked through the windows across the White House lawn to the gathering protestors there. "We've spent the last four years reshaping the world explicitly to handle something like this. Three of the enhanced are dead after illegally crossing into another country to openly defy their laws. Either step up or step down."

The room was dead silent.

Ultimately, he did what I told him to do.

The next day, Israel began shelling Abu Dis. After a few hours of bombing, they moved their military in and tested the blood of every Palestinian they found looking for traces of enhancement. For three days, they would bomb and test.

They found two more enhanced people. Each one was seized and taken to an undisclosed black site somewhere within Israel. The uproar from the international community was deafening.

That's when he stopped by.

We moved the situation room and campaign headquarters into the Oval Office. I had beds moved into the room so that Jeffery and I didn't have to leave except to use the bathroom. We needed a single location from which we could control everything.

The Iranians, Jordanians, and Syrians mobilized their forces preparing to move into Palestine. The Egyptians were trying to stay neutral, but I needed to use their territory to move our special forces into Israel in support. They secretly allowed it. The Muslim world pressured Egyptian leadership to stand against Israel, but their Brotherhood ties were stronger than silly religious ones.

Hall and I held no rallies and made no appearances while we worked to ease international tensions. We worked around the clock and were startled when the rooftop snipers began firing early yesterday morning.

They each fired off ten rounds before stopping. While the world's best marksmen wouldn't need ten shots, I was certain they had more ammunition. They simply gave up.

Hall and I stepped out onto the balcony and stood facing The Rocket. He descended from the heavens hovering just above us out of arm's reach. Venom stung the back of my throat. I loathed the vision of this man, cape floating in the heavy breeze, arms crossed in judgement, looking down on me.

"We have to stop this, Quinn," he said.

"I am the president here," Hall bellowed. Neither The Rocket nor I acknowledged his presence.

"Quinn, please."

"The Israelis should be able to determine their own fate. You have no right to stop them, and if you try, you will violate international law."

"You have got to be kidding me. Quinn!" He lowered himself enough so he could plead face to face. "This is wrong. You have to know this."

"Pious as ever!" I was enraged. "Mister Does-No-Wrong ignores reality and pretends the high ground?"

"What are you talking about, Quinn? I only ever looked up to you."

"What sort of mental gymnastics are you doing? Have you spent your life lying to yourself?" I scowled.

"You were my best friend," he said with a crack in his voice. "Then, all of a sudden, you disappeared on me."

"You have a strange memory," I said after assessing his lunacy. "You left humanity behind. You left me behind."

"I tried including you. You hated everyone so much you excluded yourself. I felt alone. You went your way. I had to go mine."

"Yeah, and your way diminished everyone. Those living in your shadow become lesser than they were."

"I never meant…"

"Of course, you didn't!" I shouted. "Of course, you didn't mean to drain your so-called loved ones of their personhood. It was a byproduct of your existence. You are moral entropy. You are the end of God's order."

"Is that what drove you into this madness? This power worship? You would endanger millions of lives because I made you feel inferior?"

I punched him. Five bones in my hand snapped against his jaw. He wasn't one of those heroes in our old comics that would roll with a punch to protect the stupid from themselves.

"This ends, Quinn," he said. "I am sorry for whatever part I played in your emotional fragility."

I heard him over my gasping in pain. I wondered if he had super vocal cords, too. "Fragility?" I snarled.

"I remember how bad your dad was. I saw it. You thought I hadn't, but I did." He paused. "Is that why you hate me?" he asked. "Because I never saved you from your father?"

His words cut deep. Of course, he was wrong, but the thought made me pause. I hadn't thought of that man in decades. "Is that why you left your mother behind? Because she couldn't protect you either?"

"Keep my mother out of your mouth," I hissed.

"I have dedicated my life to the service of my fellow man. To making the world a better place. All that money I made? I poured it into helping others. I make sure Catharine and Evie are completely taken care of."

"Who?" I asked.

"Catherine and Evie. The mom and daughter from the bridge?" Decades separated me from that night. I had no clue what their names were. He glared disbelievingly at me.

"Where are your priorities, Quinn? Where's my friend?"

I fortified myself. "Your friend overcame. Your friend rose above. My priorities are to humanity and its purity. And you… you are an impurity." I bared my teeth and watched Louis's heart break. "A threat."

"I'm stopping this. People are being hurt."

With that, he rose into the air and disappeared. A sonic boom followed.

***

I stand in the large window looking out across the lawn, past the iron gates, and to the streets beyond. The men and women sitting behind me have been running me through various scenarios and contingencies crying apocalyptic, but all I can think of is that woman pushing the stroller down the sidewalk. I wonder if the baby in there is as ugly as she is. I wonder what sort of life it'll have growing up so ugly. Weak. Would it overcome? Would it grow into the strength that I have?

Three hours ago, The Rocket landed in Abu Dis. He engaged the Israeli military. He effortlessly dismantled their weapons. He snapped guns in half. Crushed grenades. Deflected rockets. The Israelis retreated.

The wind blows the woman's hat. I enjoy watching her scramble while trying to hold the stroller still. The scene very nearly plays out like a Three Stooges bit. A man grabs the hat before it flies into traffic. He hands it to her with a smile and moves on. She pops the hat back on her head, says something to the child in the stroller, and continues walking.

The Israelis called Hall a half hour ago. Because The Rocket was ours, they wanted our help. Demanded our help. I answered for him. They would stand down and we would handle The Rocket.

Our nuclear warheads stationed on subs in the Mediterranean Sea were activated twenty minutes ago. Departmental heads and advisors were called to the office and a debate has raged for the last fifteen minutes. They wanted to reach out to The Rocket through our embassy. They wanted to show him that Israel was standing down. They wanted him home and facing a judge. It would be the best end for him.

I didn't want Louis to have the best end. He violated the law. He needed to be brought to justice.

"Quinn?" Hall calls.

My team awaits my response. I will not show weakness. Indecisiveness. I will, however, feign deliberation.

The Brotherhood is paramount. It remains my vision for a peaceful, new world. A world where humanity's fate is secure and our souls safe.

I meet eyes with Hall and nod, and he gives the order.

I am not blind to the hypocrisy of being "tough on crime." Everyone clamors to be society's protector. I understand the bigoted roots of this mantra. I know this language has been used to mask idiotic hatred of melanin so poor whites can listen to comfortable racist dog whistles and vote against their own self-interest.

I'm not like those morons.

This isn't about the hatred one human has for another. This isn't about the weak and unworthy clinging to power by villainizing the most vulnerable and marginalized. I know the righteous rightfully seize power and we have a duty to those over which we rule. We must protect them.

The enhanced aren't weak. They are not vulnerable. They're a new threat.

I step again onto the balcony. My broken hand is poorly wrapped in one of my shirts.

"The warheads have deployed," I hear from inside. In that moment, the future presents itself to me. The chaos. The retaliation. The world engulfed in war. I can see it as I have seen all things. Humanity will suffer. In the end, the righteous will survive, and a new world will be born.

With The Rocket's death, the world will understand how truly dangerous he was.

The wind blows against my arm flicking my hairs and tickling my skin. Placing my good hand on the railing, I breathe deeply and smile. I can feel my bike's handlebar grips in my hand. With my broken hand in the air, I remember those liberating summer days riding around town on adventures with Louis Bryant.

I smile the first real smile in years.

The End

9 798330 575886